York Breadcrumbs ©

York BREADCRUMBS

ISBN: 0-9543247-9-X

Published and distributed by

ENDpapers Ltd
Collage Corner, 2 Norman Court
YORK, YO1 7HU
ENGLAND
www.**endpapers**.co.uk

First published April 2005

Breath & Air text © *Helen Sant*
Back in Time text © *Ian Stuart*
Little Feet text © *Katie Ireland*
Slime & Grime text © *David Darton*

Glossary © **END**papers

Introduction © *Magdalena Chávez / Rory McCarthy*

Illustrations © **END**papers

© **END**papers

Design © *Ian Forster*

Acknowledgements

Text

Breath and Air ....Helen Sant
Back in Time ....Ian Stuart
Little Feet ....Katie Ireland
Slime and Grime ....David Darton
Editor ....Rachel Hazelwood
Glossary ....Rachel Hazelwood
Design ....Ian Forster

Illustrations

Breath and Air ....Heather Findlay/ Rachel Stainsby
Back in Time ....Rachel Stainsby
Little Feet ....Katie Street/ Richard Nagy
Slime and Grime ....Katalin Galuska
Map..Rosey Hill
Endpapers....................................Chris Utley/ Mark Withington/
Simon Micklethwaite

Production

Project Manager **END**papers ....Sally Mowbray
Project Manager
Renaissance Project ....Debbie Lovatt
Proofreader ....Ruth Wilson
Print and finish ....SPADA

Research

Historical ....Rachel Hazelwood/ Ian Stuart/
Roland Smith
Reflectors ....Mark Withington
Routes and safety ....Jim Shanks
Highways ....Terry Atkinson

Finance

ENDpapers ....Francesca Yeeles
The Renaissance Project ....Rory McCarthy

The Breadcrumbs concept ....**END**papers Ltd

ENDpapers

How to use this book ...

"Breadcrumbs" is both a stand-alone book of stories suitable for all age groups and an accompaniment to the Hansel and Gretel-like reflector trails around York.

There are three trails around York, marked on the **map** (found in the middle of the book) and marked by **reflectors** in the pavements. Each trail is split into the same four levels (see p.5) and each level tells a very different story!

Each trail has a different starting point, but together they form a complete circle. The starting points each have an artistic **installation** nearby, set into the ground.

Choose a starting point and follow the trail – before, while or after reading the stories.

When reading the stories, you will come across places, streets and objects that are highlighted in the text. These are the **"points of interest"**. (The points of interest are also marked on the map, so don't worry if you haven't had time to read the stories yet!)

Each point of interest is marked in the pavement by a **blue reflector with a collar.** When you reach one of these reflectors, check the map and it will tell you what you are looking at.

Each point of interest also has an entry in the **glossary** at the back of the book.

Attached to the pull-out map are **vouchers** that can be redeemed at shops and cafés along each trail which display the Breadcrumbs logo.

Breath & Air

Greetings! I am the Wind
and I bring you a tale ...

Back in Time

Josh Marchant crouched behind
the statue of Constantine ...

Little Feet

Time for this statue
passes ever so slowly ...

Slime and Grime

I was enjoying
my visit to York until ...

trail 1

Greetings! I am the Wind and I bring you a tale as only the Wind can. A tale carried on the back of my cooling breath, blowing through the sun-soaked air and mists of golden autumn. I travel, and you must travel with me, to the ancient city of York - to a time beyond time and a world of magic and promise.

As I speak, the leaves scurry with me and my air fairies dance and whisper to each other, their billowing cloaks of green and yellow caught up in the chase of the season. The air fairies are my messengers. They carry the power of thought as they fly.

In a wood, foxes run and hide, swallows dip

Josh Marchant crouched behind the statue of Constantine, next to the **Minster**, and was sick. Something very weird was happening to him. In his hand he held a newspaper. That wasn't strange in itself, but this was "The York Courant", not "The Yorkshire Evening Press" and the date said "July 17th 1875". One part of his mind was saying that this was all an illusion - he'd probably eaten something that disagreed with him. And the rest of his mind was saying that it was real - all of it. If he'd looked up as he sat there, trying to figure out what was going on, he would have seen that one of the gargoyles was watching him.

It had all started a couple of hours ago. He'd been going round the Minster with Mum and Fran.

Time for this statue
passes ever so slowly...

For a statue, time can be a curse -
Sat *still* all day, what could be worse?
For a life that is now history
Has no secrets, there is *no* MYSTERY.

CONSTANTINE, EMPEROR,
Never defeated,
Now forged in metal,
Forever seated
Outside the **Minster**,
Watching the people

I was enjoying my visit to York until I got hit by giant balls of ice. Until then, the only bad thing about the trip was having to listen to my horrible stepmother, Charlotte. As usual, my father had had to do something at work and had cancelled coming with us. But I was used to always coming second to his work, even when it was my birthday.

I didn't understand at all why my dad had married Charlotte. She had this false smile that she could turn into a snarl, with barely a twitch of her face muscles. This usually happened when she set eyes on me, Sarah Purecust, her ten-year-old "nuisance".

"You wilful child!" was her favourite term for me. My dad said, "It's not that bad, Sarah. It means you have a strong, determined mind. Charlotte is just worried it'll get you in trouble."

Well it didn't get me into trouble. It helped me get my own way and have a good time. I had insisted that as it was my birthday we would do what *I* wanted to do — visit the place where I was born. We had been to

and dive and squirrels fight over acorns in the dust. Old Grummety, a wizard with a very bad temper, paces up and down, scratching his head and talking to himself.

"Should I release Lucas after all this time?" he wonders. "He has been in there for five - is it years - or is it hours? I forget. Perhaps it is time to forgive him. Though he was very rude to me and he had to be punished for it. Maybe I should leave him there a little longer? He's not to be trusted. Whatever is best?"

Old Grummety takes out the glass bottle, which once held nasty medicine tasting of sprouts and wood shavings. A cure for pimples, boils and naughtiness. Old Grummety had hoped some of the traces of the sticky medicine, still clinging to the insides of the bottle, might have got into the skin of Lucas and cured his wickedness. Perhaps his rudeness too, his lying tongue and his devious nature. Perhaps not.

His Dad was at King's Manor doing some research. That was his job. He was a historian. Josh didn't fancy grubbing around in dusty old books. Old stuff was all right, but he preferred his Playstation and going to karate club. Mum and Fran had ended up in the gift shop. Josh remembered wondering why women spent so much time in shops. He had mentioned that to his sister once and she had called him a smelly little pig.

At last they emerged loaded down with carrier bags.

"Have we been long?" Fran asked innocently.

Josh said nothing.

"Come on," said Mum. "Time to meet Dad."

They had walked towards the south door, the one that was all blackened and charred from the fire years ago.

That was when it had happened.

As he stepped through the doorway, an agonising pain lanced through his head; he could see nothing but the map of red veins behind his closed eyelids.

Come and go
Come and go.

"All things I saw, all songs I sung.
All battles fought, all battles won,
I never dreamed I would be done -
Left to blister in the midday sun."

CONSTANTINE, EMPEROR,
Never defeated,
Was sick of waiting,
Forever seated
Outside the Minster,
Watching the people

Come and go
Come and go.

"But you see, the thing
that really hurts

JORVIK and then had tea at the very posh Betty's Tea Rooms, supposedly as a birthday treat, but really so that Charlotte could sit at a table by the big glass windows and be admired as a "lady" by the passers-by. I ignored her and looked up at the church across the road, St Helen's, as I helped myself to a second piece of chocolate cake.

Grummety looks at the small figure of Lucas, pressed against the glass. Lucas had been a creature of great promise - such talent, such cleverness at magic! - but so many bad habits! Once, he had been an apprentice of Grummety's but he had failed his magician's exams because he had turned the examiner into a custard tree.

Even now, Lucas stares back at Grummety through the glass, with a huffy look in his eyes, as though he might at any moment blow a raspberry at the old wizard. But he seems to realise this really isn't the time to do so.

Grummety sets the bottle down. "Shall I -

And then the pain was gone, and he was standing on the steps, looking down at the crowd milling around Minster Gates. A horse and carriage rumbled slowly past. Coach ride round the city. Brilliant. They were going to do that tomorrow.

A lot of the women were wearing long skirts and bonnets. Must be one of those - what do you call them? - re-enactment groups.

But as he looked round he realised that *everyone* was wearing old-fashioned costume - and they hadn't been when he'd gone into the Minster. Then he noticed the smells...a stomach-turning mixture of coal smoke, horse muck and sweat. That was the moment he saw the newspaper and knew he was going to be sick.

Josh felt a hand on his shoulder.

"You all right, mate?"

The boy was Josh's age, but his face was thin and grey with fatigue. He was wearing boots too big for him and no socks.

"I've got to get out of here!" Josh sobbed. "I've got to get back to my mum and my sister!"

"Haven't we all, mate," said the boy quietly,

Is KIDS!
They all drive me BERSERK!
They poke me, stroke me,
climb and kick me.
They drip ice cream and make
me sticky!"

CONSTANTINE, EMPEROR,
Never defeated!
At the hands of CHILDREN
Now being treated
Like he doesn't count!

Watching the people
Come and go
Come and go.

"When I walked the Earth
in olden days,"

Daydreaming afterwards, I didn't realise we had walked to the Minster and I was going to be in for an earful of history and God stuff. As Charlotte droned on at my younger brother, I wandered off across the street to look at an old **Roman column** of stones, imagining that it was covering an ancient rocket that had brought aliens to earth to

han't I?" he asks himself again. He looks at Lucas, an elf with brown hair, twinkling eyes, feathered hat and white jerkin with medicine stains on. Grummety sighs.

"I suppose now is as good a time as any." And with that, he uncorks the bottle, and Lucas flies out of his prison, flutters to the ground and then grows bigger and bigger until he is almost as tall as Grummety himself.

"Master," says Lucas, bowing, but unable to resist a cheeky grin. "To what do I owe this honour?"

Grummety shuffles his feet and looks about him. He is, after all, the proudest magician in all of York.

"You are free to go Lucas," he says.

"Oh - how wonderful Master!" Lucas skips from side to side, twirling round the trees and kicking up the piles of fallen leaves.

"Now don't go making any mischief,"

"but that's not as easy as it might be."

Josh noticed that the boy kept looking anxiously down Minster Gates.

"Thing is," he said, "I've got to get out of here as well...smartish...Oh my God!" The boy clamped his hand on Josh's arm. "He's seen us! Up! Come on! Get up! Or he'll nab the pair of us!"

Constantine says,
wishing for praise,
"Children were nice,
polite and clean,
They NEVER EVER ate ICE CREAM!

start the human race.

In the growing winter darkness I hadn't noticed the storm clouds. Suddenly, a sharp crack of lightning hit the top of the column and a shower of sparks rained over me, making me feel strange and tingly. Then came hailstones - sharp blocks of ice that hammered into me. As they got bigger and bigger they knocked me onto my back. Everything went out of focus. I could hear the pounding feet of people running for cover. Over all the noise came my stepmother's terrible screeching, "Where are you, you stupid, wilful child? Come here at once!"

What? Why couldn't she see me? She could usually see me even when I was behind her. I looked up. Hurtling towards me was a hailstone the size of my head. Either this was the worst storm in history or... or I was getting smaller. What was going on? I rolled out of its way straight into a river of rushing rainwater. As I tried to scramble to my feet, a giant shoe came crashing down from the

11

finishes Grummety to himself, as Lucas disappears off into the distance, flying with me, the Wind, through the air, and shouting with delight.

"Too late," says Grummety sadly. "I fear I have made a mistake. Now he'll be causing trouble all over York. Oh well, what will go around will come around."

Grummety smoothes his beard by way of comfort, and settles down under a tree for an afternoon nap.

Meanwhile, Lucas has made himself smaller again. He is the kind of elf called a shape-shifter. He can make himself into anything he chooses. He can also hide in things like statues and make them come alive.

"I am free!" he mutters to himself, as he travels alongside me, making faces at the air fairies, who are shocked and scared by him. The air fairies are delicate. Mirabelle one of the eldest, screams as Lucas pushes

Josh peered down the street, shading his eyes against the sun. Nothing. Then he felt it. It was as though a shadow had fallen across his heart. He shivered.

The boy walked a couple of paces then cried out in pain.

"Only you got to help me!" he said. "Done me ankle in...Can't walk too good." He waved at the big house at the east end of

'Please,' they said
and 'thank you,' too,
Cleaned the chariots, without ado.
They ONLY spoke when spoken to
And always washed
when asked to do.

CONSTANTINE, EMPEROR,
Never defeated!
Just like a FOOL –
That's how I'm treated!
Forever to sit

Watching those CHILDREN
COME AND GO
COME AND GO!"

sky. I *had* shrunk. How could this be happening? A swirling stream of water came hurtling towards me and I bodysurfed it until it swept me into a nearby drain.

I plunged down in a torrential waterfall and hit the bottom of a pipe before being pounded along, struggling to keep afloat. Just when I was sure I was going to drown,

I bounced downwards through a small hole and landed in a pool of muddy water.

I recovered my breath and stood up, feeling bruised all over and very frightened. I put my right hand out to steady myself and the wall felt soft and squelchy. There was movement all around me. It was creepy; all the hairs on my body stood on end. As my

her off her cloud. She falls through billows of feathery air, regains her balance, and half flies, half tumbles onto a fresh cloud, next to me.

"Who is that horrible imp, Mister Wind?" she cries.

"It's only Lucas," I reply. "He's an elf, not an imp - a mischief maker it's true - not everyone's favourite person."

"Well, he's evil!" declares Mirabelle, pouting, as she straightens her wings. "He's got a wicked glint in his eye. I don't like him one bit!"

I chuckle as I snatch a woman's shopping list out of her hand and make it fly across

the Minster. "If we can get there...they say there's someone there who looks after the likes of us."

Josh put his arm round the boy's shoulder and together they hobbled round the **Queen's Path**. All the time Josh could sense something searching for them, reaching out like a beam of black light.

"A gate..." the boy was muttering..."They said there is a gate..."

"Is this it?"

"Got to be." The boy reached skilfully through the bars of the gate and flicked up the latch. Then they were through and hurrying round to the back of the house.

There was a window with wooden shutters

After this outburst
day turns to night,
Constantine uses all of his might,
To heave himself off
his cold, hard chair,
To seek an army of men
somewhere.

The windows shudder and
chimney tops judder
As Constantine clomp-stomps past.

The beat of his boots
shakes the trees

eyes adjusted to the gloom, it looked as though the walls were breathing. I realised that they were full of a mass of worms and spiders and slug-like creatures moving slowly through the earth. I shuddered and quickly removed my hand. I was shaking, unable to believe what was happening.

After a few minutes, I forced myself to calm

down and think. I may have been the height of a Barbie doll, but at least I was alive. Maybe I could find a way out. I could feel a gentle wind coming from a small crevice in front of me. I clambered up and dropped down into a much larger tunnel. It was gloomy, but there must be a way out if there was a breeze. I started to move

forward, feeling a bit more confident, when suddenly I heard a loud hiss from behind me. I froze. Petrified.

I turned round very, very slowly.

At first, all I could see were two bright eyes, about a foot from me. Gradually, the rest came into focus. It was a rat. A giant rat. I stumbled back a step, trembling. The rat

the ground. She squeals and runs after it, then stops, looking around embarrassed. I stop and let her catch up with the tatty paper. We're outside the **Minster**, the biggest and oldest cathedral in York.

I watch as Lucas takes up his place at the south side of York **Minster** and disappears into one of the gargoyles, chuckling to

himself, dreaming up pranks to play on the people below.

Standing on the street, doing nothing in particular, is Matthew Trimble, a fair-haired child with a curiosity that leads him to explore high places. He likes to be near the sky and the clouds. He is very naughty and

and steps going down to a basement. Half a dozen geese were pecking at the dirt. The two boys stopped in their tracks. The geese turned their long necks to look at the intruders and then exploded into a chorus of cackling and hissing and beating wings.

The basement door flung back on its hinges and a plump woman with a red face came running up the steps.

lazy too. He hides just to get out of doing any work in his parents' shop, or worse, his schooling. But Matthew's most terrible habit is being mean to animals.

He likes nothing better than to kick a passing dog or chase after the pigeons and pull out their feathers. I know all about

"What are you two doing here!" she roared.

Josh looked helplessly at his companion. The boy limped forward.

"Please miss, I'm Tom Franks...I'm from the Institute...I'm on the run..."

"Show me your hands."

The boy held out his hands, palms upwards. Josh looked in horror. Burned deep into the palm of the boy's right hand were two

to their roots
the gargoyles look on aghast!

Turning the corner Constantine spies
**A tall sundial where
four lions lie.**

Each a handsome, fearsome beast
At North and South, West and East.

"Right, clean your whiskers,
brush off your paws,
Swish your long tails,
sharpen your claws!

Come with me all the
way to Rome.
We leave right now
and there you shall roam!"

was rigid, its muscles taut, ready for a fight. Its whiskers twitched. Drool seeped out of the closed mouth in anticipation of eating me. My legs began to buckle. The rat opened its mouth into a snarl that even my stepmother would have been proud of.

The rat sprang forward. I was frozen in shock. A sharp claw dug deep into my

Matthew. Lucas grins through the face of the gargoyle. He sees Matthew and in one glance he knows too. I watch Lucas watching Matthew. And it seems as if Lucas senses Matthew is a boy who can be led into further mischief. Lucas calls to Matthew in a silvery voice.

"Matthew Trimble, there are lots of plump pigeons up on this roof for you to tease and worry. Why don't you take a closer look?"

Matthew hears Lucas and looks around, frowning. He shrugs. Why not? He begins to climb. Even I – the all-seeing Wind – can't bear to look.

What is Lucas up to?

---

letters - VS.

The woman took the boy's hand gently and closed his fingers. "You're all right now, love," she said. "Come into the kitchen. I'll look after the pair of you."

A bowl of beef stew can work wonders. Josh picked a shred of meat from between his teeth and stared into the glowing coals of the fire. The kitchen was warm and safe; he

felt better than he had all day. He looked round at the rows of gleaming copper pans and what looked like a giant barbecue spit over the fire. The kitchen smelled of polished wood and burnt milk. It was real, then - all of it. How was he going to explain it all to Mum and Dad and Fran?

How could he even begin? And how on earth was he going to get back?

"Ouch!"

The woman was wrapping a bandage round Tom's ankle. From their conversation Josh gathered that her name was Lizzie Thurcross, housekeeper to Doctor Wheldrake. The doctor was often away and Lizzie had the house to herself most of the time.

Lizzie turned to Josh. "You're a quiet one.

"But we're quite content here
where we are
Under the sun, the moon
and bright star,
As each by turn a shadow
does throw
So that all of York
the time will know.

We lions four
Forever seated
Under a sundial –
Never mistreated.

---

shoulder. I screamed. The teeth loomed above me, coming closer and closer. I stopped breathing.

I knew I was going to die.

But the bite never came. I sensed hot breath on my neck as a strong force knocked the rat hard to the left, ripping its claw from my shoulder. I tumbled onto my back and

looked around, anxious to see what had saved me.

I wished I hadn't. If the rat had seemed big, the black beast that now stood above me was huge. Even bigger teeth were visible in the panting mouth, where the bloody remains of the rat were dripping. Its bright green eyes sized me up as it got ready for a

second kill.

It had gone deadly quiet. My heart sounded like African drums. But the creature made no move. Then a high-pitched, strangely tuneful whistle pierced the silence. A black paw gently lifted me and I was thrown up and spun round, so that I landed astride the animal's back facing its ears. The ears of a

Meanwhile, the air fairies have moved on ahead, jostling each other playfully, past **St William's College**. They stop and tap at the Tudor windows, smiling and calling to the ghost who lives in the top room. They quickly become bored and fly away to Gillygate, where Matthew's parents live, Jacob and Liza Trimble.

We don't even know your name."

"Josh."

"Show me your hands." Lizzie sniffed. "He's not branded you then..."

"He just helped me," said Tom quickly. "Spall was on my tail. I reckon we can trust him."

"Where are you from?" said Lizzie.

"North London."

"That's all right. I was worried you might be one of Spall's sneaks."

"Who is this Spall?"

"He's the very devil himself," whispered Tom. "Straight from the fires of Hell."

Lizzie nodded. "Maybe he's not so far wrong either. He came to York five years ago...no one knows where from...but he bought this big house down Andrewgate and

opened it up as an orphanage. Offered to take thirty city orphans off the council's hands - for a price of course - and turn them into honest tradesmen. The council were delighted. But then there are...stories."

Josh shifted in his chair. "What stories?"

"Well," said Lizzie, "they seem to have a terrible lot of sickness down Andrewgate, and the ones who don't die of fever run

We like to sit
And watch the people
Come and go
Come and go."

Constantine, cross,
stamp-tramps up the street –
He will not accept this silly defeat.
Wild and mad he moves
through the night –

Even Ogleforth Ogre
himself takes fright!

The emperor turns left
and on he strides
Up to the place where
the **Roman road** hides.

huge black cat. I felt like I was going to have a heart attack. It was all too much. I just wanted to go home, even to Charlotte.

The cat started to move forward and I sensed a presence behind me, the source of the whistling, which now stopped. I turned slowly.

The thing that sat behind me was truly

Jacob is a stout man with a runaway tongue and Liza is thin and quiet and often just smiles rather than speaks. Together they run a shoemakers' shop.

The air fairies cluster at the window of the Trimbles' house. It is just about teatime, and Liza has laid the table with bread,

brambles and roasted potatoes. Matthew is late and his parents are worrying about where he is. Just then there is a knock at the door. Liza answers it to see Father Lafferty's cross face and his hand at Matthew's collar.

"Oh, Father - what's he done now?" she says.

"I caught your boy climbing on the Minster again," says the priest gruffly. "Trying to frighten the birds, he was. He could have fallen and broken his neck if I hadn't been there, you know. It's a disgrace! The boy thinks he's in a penny fair!"

"Oh, I'm sorry Father, it won't happen again," says Liza. "He's a - he just wanted to

away...'

"They never!" said Tom. "He done them in!"

"You know that for certain?"

Tom was staring into the fire.

"He sends us out robbing," he said. "The ones that are fit enough, that is. He gets paid twice, you see, once from the council and again from what we bring in. That's

how I did my ankle. I was doing one of them houses in Micklegate. Landed badly when I jumped from the window."

"But you've never seen him kill anyone?" Lizzie persisted.

"You're all right as long as you keep your health," said Tom, fighting to keep his voice steady, "but if you fall ill, then he tells you that you're going on a little visit – 'Time you

Here ghosts of soldiers
all still stand –
Five thousand awaiting their
final command.

"Follow me, men!
Straddle your horses!
It's time you and I all joined forces.

Onwards and upwards,
just wait and see –
If we fight as one,
we shall be free!"

"We died in battle –
we've played our parts."

The soldiers cry,
"there's peace in our hearts.
You cannot budge us ghosts,
your Grace,
Now we have York
as our resting place."

disgusting. First I saw its left leg. Grey-green mould hung off brown bones. I shuddered and slowly raised my eyes. Above the waist, the mould was interspersed with what looked like human skin. I could even make out some features. My eyes flicked right and I could see an arm and leg that were in much better shape.

Definitely human.

Down the left side of the head was shoulder-length glowing blonde hair. The left side of the face under the hair was, however, a foul, flaking mess, with a grotesquely blood-veined eye sunk into a socket within the skull. In contrast, the nose was almost normal and the right side of the

head was that of a once-obviously handsome teenager, though the hair on this side was mouldy straw.

I turned away from the revolting sight behind me and gripped the hair behind the cat's ears as we picked up speed. Delayed shock set in and I felt the tears coming. I tried to hold them back, but then all I could

be closer to God, Father."

"Then bring the boy to church!" says Father Lafferty.

"Yes Father, we'll see you this Sunday. And thank you for rescuing him," Liza says timidly. Jacob sits by the fire, polishing his boots and pretending to be elsewhere. She

glances in his direction, but he says nothing.

Father Lafferty snorts, releases Matthew from his grasp and goes on his way.

"Oh Matthew, what are you thinking of?" says Liza as her son runs to her.

"I just like it on 'igh, mother, I weren't doing

went to see your auntie in Scarborough,' he says. I've heard him say that to three of my mates. None of them came back from Scarborough. That's why I ran away when I did my ankle in - I'd be no use to him now..."

The bright coals shifted in the grate; Josh could smell the sharp tang of sulphur.

"Nobody can prove a thing, you see," said Lizzie. "He's untouchable. Vincent Spall is

afraid of nothing on God's earth."

"That's not true," said Tom quietly. "He's afraid of the light. No one's ever seen his face - not in full daylight. He never has more than one candle lit in his room, and when you go and see him, his face is always in the shadow."

"Doesn't he ever go out?" said Josh.

"Not if he can help it. If he has to go out in

the day he wears a black silk mask over his face."

"I've seen him once," said Lizzie. "I thought he had a disease."

"He does," said Tom, "he's eaten from the inside by evil..."

"He must want you very much," said Josh, "if he's out in the sunlight..."

Constantine couldn't
believe his ears.
"COWARDS!" he yelled,
almost in tears.
For buried deep down lived a fear,
That grew inside him
year after year.

The truth was he was so, so lonely
Tired of being the one and only
Big emperor around who
was condemned
To live through his life
without a friend.

do was let it come out in sobbing floods.

Eventually, my crying slowed and I was shocked to hear a voice behind me.

"It's all right, I know it's difficult. I was terrified when we first came down here. You sort of get used to it." The voice was impossibly tender for the gross thing that sat behind me.

"It must be your birthday today?" There were a million things I needed to ask this — whatever it was — and it was going on about my birthday! My fear made me angry.

"What on earth does it matter if it is my birthday?"

"Oh, it matters. You wouldn't be here

no 'arm," says Matthew, scowling. (He decides not to mention the strange voice from on high…)

"You're a funny lad," says Jacob.

"Oh, now you speak," says Liza. "You never says a word when old Lafferty's stood there telling us off for not going to church."

Jacob stands up and stretches. "It's nowt to worry about, lass," he says. "Besides, there's more important things to fret about. Like that."

He indicates with his head in the direction of the squeaking and scratching noise from the corner of the room.

"Rats," says Jacob. "We need to sort 'em out. Time we got a cat I think."

"But I don't like cats," says Liza timidly.

"Neither do I," says Matthew, "unless I can pull their tails."

"Now then, Matthew, don't be cruel," says his mother. "Anyway, we don't need a real

"He can't afford to let any of us escape. Not one. Or the truth might come out."

"Why on earth don't you go to the police?" said Josh.

Lizzie and Tom looked at him in disbelief. "You mean the constables?"

"Yes."

"And what good would that do? There are

three of them for the whole of York. Two of those are always drunk and the other one's asleep."

Lizzie turned to Tom. "You've got to get out of York, young Tom. I'd keep you here but the doctor's back tonight and I can't be caught with a stowaway in the house. But I've got a sister at Malton - married to a farmer. If you could get out to her, I know you'd be all right..."

EMPEROR CONSTANTINE
Never defeated,
Now all ALONE,
Feeling mistreated.

He no longer wants
To watch the people
Come and go
Come and go.

Constantine feels a heavy sadness
Added to which is
his usual badness.
Daffodils are crushed
under his feet,

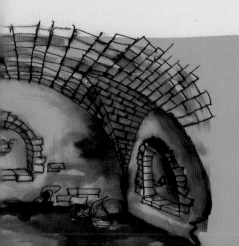

otherwise."

Before I could enquire further, the temperature dropped suddenly and the shadows seemed to shift out of line with our motion.

"Grim is close," came a whisper from behind me. "Fly, Snickel, fly." The cat shot forward. I nearly fell and clung on to the fur

desperately, ducking at dips in the tunnel roof. Suddenly, ahead of us was a wall of stone and we were flying straight into it. I screamed.

"It's all right. It's the foundations of Monk Bar."

It didn't reassure me and I closed my eyes as the wall of stones rushed up to meet us. At

cat. We can get a stone one."

"What's a stone one gonna do?" says Jacob. "You daft mare - you don't believe that old wives' tale, do you?"

There was an old belief in York that to have a stone cat upon the roof of one's home was to keep it free from mice and rats, as good as having a real cat. But Jacob is a man of

reality.

"I'm going to go and see my mate the rat-catcher," he says, "and get us a mouse-killer!"

Well now, two sunsets and two blustery journeys pass for the air fairies and me. We have been following Lucas who has been

"I don't stand a chance," said Tom miserably, "not with my leg. He'll catch me and take me back to the Institute and then he'll send me to Scarborough!"

Josh thought of that dark presence he had sensed by the Minster. Tom had got them away from that. And now they were both in the same boat. He stared at the framed map of York on the wall. Then the idea came to

him out of the air, fresh, new minted, gleaming.

"I know how we can do it," he said.

Josh had never been out in the moonlight before. Everything was so bright, and yet so unreal. House fronts, gable ends and chimney pots were splashed at random with a silver wash of light. Only the Minster

as he sniffs and sulks
down the street.

He stamps along the
pavements of York,
All the way up the
Lord Mayor's Walk.

Up Gillygate he turns,
now in tears
As he can see only long
lonely years.

"That's it – it's over –
I shan't make Rome.
I just can't do it all on my own.
The magic that brought me to life
Is vanishing now, with the
coming light.

the last moment, I felt us veer sharply to the left and down. A mouldy arm gripped my right side to prevent me from slipping off.

We emerged from a narrow passage into a wide tunnel and slowed. The temperature rose again and the cat came to a stop.

"I sense that Grim has a real need for you…" His voice faded out.

I was sick of this. I needed to know what was going on.

"Who – or what – the hell is Grim? Why does he want me and more to the point, why and how am I here anyway? And come to that, who – or, excuse my bluntness – *what* are you?"

"I sometimes forget…" He sighed. "Before I

following Matthew. He has a plan for that boy but he won't tell us what it is. Matthew is playing at being a Viking, pretending that the wild men of York, the **stone figures on top of Monk Bar**, are the enemy, ready to storm the city. He launches an attack, using apple cores, pebbles and his deadliest secret weapon, horse chestnut cases fired as catapults and filled with black treacle. Lucas, watching Matthew from his hiding place in one of the wild men statues, uses his magic to catch a chestnut case and throw it at Jim Jones who is delivering beer on his horse-drawn cart. It frightens poor Jim so much that he nearly crashes into the side of the bar walls. Jim chases Matthew down **Lord Mayor's Walk** and up Gillygate as far as the Trimbles' shop. Furious and dripping treacle, he asks what their son is doing running amok when he should be earning his keep?

Lucas, watching from a nearby chimney

was untouched, a cliff of darkness reaching up to the stars.

Lizzie kissed Tom on the forehead.

"Safe journey," she whispered, "and if that devil Spall asks any questions, he'll get nothing from me."

She turned to Josh.

"Take care of yourself. You're a rum 'un.

Different somehow. Perhaps it's living in North London."

"Perhaps," said Josh.

"Good luck to the pair of you."

Josh's heart was thumping in his chest.

"Light the torch."

Tom flicked at something like an old fashioned cigarette lighter and an orange

My will has gone,
no hope in my soul.
I suddenly feel so tired and old."
Now, at last
in Exhibition Square -
He falls and rests
in the water there.

As the pale gold sun begins to rise
The emperor shuts his metal eyes.
He thinks he's lost the battle now
He wants to give up,
to take his bow.

became part of the half-dead down here, I was Mark. I was sixteen, 126 years ago today, when we — my twin sister, Rachel, and I — came down."

"Half-dead? Am I going to become like you?" I dreaded the answer.

"And like Snickel here. You probably haven't noticed that he is a little decayed too,

although luckily his legs remain strong. He has no tail at all, just the bone, which really upsets him. He was the original York alley cat you know. The one that gave its name to Snickelway — the local word for the narrow passages that at one time were the roaming grounds of the alley cats. He was with us when we were...when we came down."

What on earth was he going on about? And who was this Grim? I wasn't absolutely sure whether we had been racing away from him or towards him. I wasn't convinced I wanted to know either, but I knew I had to ask. Just as I was about to, however, the tunnel we were in began to echo to the sound of marching feet.

top, chuckles.

Liza punishes Matthew by setting him to work on pulling all the rusty nails out of the oldest and smelliest shoes, even though Matthew swears blind it wasn't he who had attacked Jim Jones. Then, in walks Jacob with a mewing bundle under his arm, which does nothing to cheer the lad up.

He hates cats so! Jacob pulls back the folds of the woollen blanket and reveals the whiskers and furry face beneath.

"Oh, what a cute kitten!" Liza says, as she admires his black and white coat and soft golden eyes.

"It's not a kitten Missus," says Jacob. "It's a fearsome mouse- and rat-catcher."

"Oh, let's call him Fluffy," says Liza.

"Woman! He already has a name," Jacob says. "He's called Domino."

"That's not a fighter's name," says Matthew. "I'd 'ave called him Eric Bloodaxe."

"That's enough of that Viking talk," Liza

light flared in the darkness. He held it to the wooden stave wrapped in rags until the flame took hold.

"He'll be close," murmured Josh, "so we don't even try to hide. Hold the torch near your face and make sure that he can see it's you. I'll hang back in the shadows. Once we're in Monkgate...what's that little lane on the left...near **Monk Bar**?"

"**Elbow Lane**".

"We split up there. You give me the torch. You go through the bar and head for the Malton Road. I'll lead him up **Lord Mayor's Walk** and then...I'll think of something..." he added lamely.

The torchlight swung crazily across Tom's face.

"You're a good mate, Josh. A good mate."

WILLIAM ETTY
1787–1849

Under the fountain,
Broken and beaten –

CONSTANTINE, EMPEROR
Was at last
Defeated...

But some true magic is
still at work
In the fresh air of ye olde York.
The fountain tinkles
and dawn cracks through
The spirit of change wakes
in the dew.

"What's that?" I shouted above the rising sound. I looked around. The tunnel was lined with a proper floor of deliberately placed stones. "Where are we?"

"This is the old **Roman road** out of the city. I'd forgotten the date, midwinter's day. The lost Roman legion is due through about now."

Right on cue, in amazing colour, came the soldiers. Snickel whimpered and moved back out of the way quickly as the ghostly parade passed with flags and trumpeters and swords all visible, but silent apart from the pounding feet.

"This regiment mysteriously died as it left York and their spirits have been down here

says. "We've had quite enough of *that* today."

She begins to fuss over Domino, much to Matthew's disgust. He eyes the cat spitefully. As Liza disappears to fetch a saucer of milk, Matthew grabs Domino's tail and pulls hard. Domino looks alarmed and

hides under the table. Lucas, still watching from across the road, decides something needs to be done about this naughty little boy. As he crosses the road, his shadow is the shape of a cat...

A week later, the Trimbles are still troubled by vermin. When a brave little mouse dares

---

Spall was waiting for them on College Green. Josh could see nothing beyond the flames of the torch, but he sensed that cold, fierce presence, watching him from the darkness. A cloud slid from the face of the moon; the grass was tipped by silver, and there, standing by the **sundial**, was the figure of a man, with one booted foot on the seat. Josh could see nothing of his features; it was as though the darkness had

congealed into human shape.

Though they were fifteen yards away, walking down College Street, they could hear him breathing - a slow, sibilant hiss. He spoke.

"I want you back, Tom Franks."

Tom's pace faltered for a moment and the torch in his hand started to shake.

"Don't listen!" hissed Josh, willing him on. "It's just a voice in the dark! Go on!"

Tom stumbled round the corner into Goodramgate with Josh close behind him.

"Run!" said Josh. "We've got to gain some ground!"

The towers of **Monk Bar** loomed up in front of them. "Quick! In here!" said Josh. The two boys plunged into the wide

---

William Etty now looks down,
A statue himself, and with a frown
Considers Constantine in his woe,
Then pokes him hard with
his stone toe.

Constantine groans
and lifts his hand –
"Leave me alone,
you foul little man.
I want to die – I'm feeling tearful.
I shan't let you
make me be cheerful."

---

ever since," whispered Mark. "At least it is not completely lonely here."

The soldiers looked vacantly ahead, but one, midway through the ranks, turned as he passed and seemed to stare right at me. I nearly fell off Snickel with surprise. The soldier who stared at me forlornly looked exactly like my grandfather did in an old

black and white photo we had of him as a young man. I had often heard him say that the Purecusts had been in York since Roman times. But this freaked me out.

"I don't want to be here. And I certainly don't want to be like you." My voice rose in horror at the thought.

"Thanks a lot."

"I didn't mean..."

"It's all right. I know. There are two ways out. Over the years, two have escaped by using a chant that returns them to the upper world. But it's not easy to get out. Especially when Grim wants you so bad..."

"And the other way out?"

to cross the floor right in front of Jacob's nose, he yells at Domino, "What does tha think tha's doing! It's a mouse! Kill it!"

Domino winks at the bold little creature and makes a running leap for the highest shelf in the room. There he stays, secretly grinning to himself. "What the - did you see that? Jacob exclaimed.

Matthew laughs. "A cat who's afraid of mice!" he keeps saying. Jacob looks about to explode with rage.

"I don't believe this is 'appening to me!" he wails.

"Well," says Liza, "he's still a lovely cat."

"Lovely cat! Lovely cat!" Jacob says in a voice that is now purple with temper. "I didn't want a pet, woman! I wanted a killer!" He grabs his coat and makes for the door. "I'm going to see that rat-catcher Barney," he says crossly, "to sort this out!"

Matthew is still laughing about it the next day - Saturday - the busiest day for the shop

opening of **Elbow Lane** and stood with their backs to the wall, gasping for breath.

"Give me the torch!" said Josh. "And go!"

Tom handed him the torch. For a moment they stood face to face. Tom held out his hand.

"Thanks," he said. "Thanks."

They shook hands, and Josh felt the rough skin of the boy's disfigured palm, then Tom

"Calm down dear Sir!
I know you're upset
I've heard how lonely you can get.
Listen, friend, before you give in
Let me help you smile, lift up
your chin!

"Look in the water,
pick up a penny –
Choose one you like,
for there are many.
Quickly now! The sun rises soon
And we'll stay like this
'til next full moon."

"To let Grim have you."

"What does that mean? Who is this Grim?" Mark was about to answer when the shadows shifted again, like they were independent of the things they were attached to. He hesitated, but I needed to know.

"Who is this Grim?" I repeated.

"I am your blood." The deep, gravelly voice was dripping with so much menace that I could hardly make out the words.

"You could be the one!" Mark's voice sounded strangely excited, but then he added, "We have to get you out of here."

Behind the departing Roman soldiers it suddenly got terribly dark. A shadow began to cover the whole tunnel and fingers o ice-cold air began stabbing at me. Grim slowly appeared in the distant tunnel entrance. Decaying flesh hung over bones. There was no sign of skin, just a heaving mass of gore, rippling as he advanced slowly but purposefully towards us. With sudden and surprising speed, out of the

when all of York come in to have their shoes repaired. The brazen rats and mice poke their heads out from underneath pieces of old leather lying on the counter, frightening women of a certain age.

'This can't go on,' says Liza in despair as one of their best customers, Mrs

was away, clattering through the stone archway of the bar.

Josh waited until Tom's footsteps had died away, then ran back into Monkgate. As he glanced at the torch fizzing and crackling in his hand, he slipped on the cobbles and fell heavily.

Next thing he knew, a man was standing over him. This is what it's like, thought Josh,

this is what happens when you die. It can't get any worse than this. He made himself look up. Spall was wearing a long black cloak; there was a hint of lace at the wrists and neck, and the lower half of his face was covered by what looked like a tissue of cobwebs.

For a moment Spall looked as surprised as Josh. "Where is he?" he hissed, lunging

Cottlestone, runs out the shop screaming, a rat with large teeth in hot pursuit.

"Well Barney should be here any minute now love," says Jacob, confidently.

"Not another cat, Dad?" says Matthew sulkily, trying to pull Domino's tail without anyone seeing. The cat snarls at him and

Constantine does
what Etty has told:
Picks up a coin, feeling quite bold.
He stands,
he thinks that he is dreaming
He feels a thousand
different feelings.

For every penny shows the parts
Of all that lives in
children's hearts:
Each of the coins thrown
over the years
Keeps secret all their hopes
and fears.

mass of slime came what must have been an arm, huge long spindles of fingers reaching out for me.

Snickel was suddenly moving. Grim missed me by millimetres as we fled. I turned to watch him squeezing through the opening behind us, evil eyes watching me. Snickel went even faster, his breath short, painful

digs him with a claw. Matthew squeals and moves away. He's sure there's something funny about that cat; he just can't put his finger on it. Meantime, my air fairies and I are clustered outside and watching through the window, wondering what Lucas is up to. We look on as Barney the rat-catcher enters the shop.

"Good morning," says Jacob.

He looks around, and then in puzzlement at Barney. "Well, where is she?" he asks eagerly.

"She's here, Jacob. In this parcel."

"What? There's never a cat in there!"

"No, no Jacob, there is - she's a stone cat Matilda."

"What!? What are you talking about, man? I asked you to get us a real cat. One that *isn't* afraid of mice."

"Well, it's Matilda and she's a good luck mascot, Jacob."

---

forward.

Josh flung himself sideways and scrambled to his feet. His mind switched off and his body took over. He had practised this hundreds of times every Thursday at karate club. As Spall slid past, Josh tried an elbow jab, which did not connect. Suddenly he was smothered in the folds of Spall's cloak and retching at the smell of perfume and decay. Bony fingers grasped his wrist. Grunting, Josh managed to pivot on one foot and kick out wildly. It connected somewhere because Spall gave a little cough of annoyance and his grip slackened for an instant. It was enough. Josh got in another kick and a straight arm jab and he was away, under Monk Bar. The last thing Josh heard as he turned the corner into **Lord Mayor's Walk** was the sound of Spall cursing as he got to his feet.

Josh was young and fit, and opened up a good lead. He pounded along Lord Mayor's Walk with ten thousand stars lurching crazily above his head and one thought filling his mind - "How do I get home?"

But then the pace began to tell. His legs began to ache and he slowed. But then he heard a noise behind him - the steady "tap

---

He finds he can read and understand
The coins he holds in his cold hands.
This boy longs to drive a train,
This girl wants to fly a plane.
One child wishes she could be taller.
Another wishes
his ears were smaller.

But one says he'd like
nothing more
Than to grow to be
a great emperor.
To be wise, and just,
and true, and kind –
It's Constantine he has in mind

---

wheezes. The tunnel roof dipped and it was wet and thick with mud. Mark whistled and grabbed hold of me as Snickel suddenly leaped upwards and buried us in the sludgy ceiling of the tunnel, almost suffocating me. He placed my hands around some roots sticking through.

"Hold on." I heard Snickel drop from beneath us and dash off to our right.

"Where are we?" I choked.

"Under the **moat** that used to run in front of the city wall, near the surface. Grim finds it difficult to detect us within the mud. Ssssh."

Again it was icy cold. I heard Grim stop

"You stupid fool!" Jacob is getting annoyed. "I don't believe in that nonsense! Do I look like my brain's cooked?"

Barney shifts his weight from one foot to the other, trying to think of an answer.

"Now take that heap of stone and–"

"Wait a minute," says his wife. "Don't be so hasty. Let's see her."

"Her? It's a statue, woman!" says Jacob. He groans to himself as Barney unwraps the paper.

Beneath the folds of crinkly paper lies an elegant white statue of a cat with green eyes, just a bit bigger than a real cat.

"Oh, that's perfect," says Liza. Matthew scowls at it. No point in pulling its tail. "You like climbing up high places, boy. You can help us put her on the roof," she says. So Barney, Liza and Matthew carry the **white stone cat** between them and, after a clambering of the ladder and a little hammering, Matilda the stone cat

---

tap" of Spall's boots as he closed the distance between them. Josh dragged the air into his lungs in great gulps and staggered on. Something wet and sticky was trickling down his arm. Every stride was agony. It felt as though the pavement was melting under his feet. Even the buildings seemed to crumble and re-shape themselves, like a speeded up film.

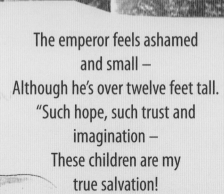

The emperor feels ashamed
and small –
Although he's over twelve feet tall.
"Such hope, such trust and
imagination –
These children are my
true salvation!

From now on, I promise to be
All that they are, just, true –
and FREE!"
Constantine smiles.
The battle is won.
He stretches himself
beneath the sun.

---

below us. I stopped breathing. Slurp. A bony finger sliced through the sludge, less than a centimetre from my head. Then I heard Snickel snarl some way off. Grim growled and I sensed him move off in Snickel's direction.

"Don't worry. Snickel always gets away."

I couldn't hold on any more. I slipped, squelching, and dropped to the tunnel floor. Mark came down awkwardly beside me.

"Snickel will lead Grim close to his favourite lair. He can never resist a visit to the surface. It may give us a chance."

"Where's his lair?"

"It's in the **locked tower** at the corner of the city walls. It's the only place for some reason that Grim can go a little way above the ground. I suppose because it is completely sealed in. He thinks one day he'll be able to get out. So he broods in there, making it particularly chilly for the tourists just above on the city walls."

decorates the roof of their shop in Gillygate. Quick as a wink, Lucas leaps into the statue. At that moment, Domino wakes up from what feels like a very long sleep and creeps out from under a bed. Hungry. And slightly confused. The air fairies, looking at Lucas, shake their heads in dismay.

"What's Lucas up to, Mister Wind?" says Mirabelle to me. "What's he going to do to that little boy?"

"I fear he's going to teach Matthew a lesson," I say. The air fairies look at me in disbelief and flap their wings in protest.

"Matthew Trimble," calls Lucas in his silvery tone.

Matthew jumps and looks around "Matthew Trimble," calls Lucas again Matthew looks up at the stone cat, who winks at him. Frightened, he asks,

"Who are you? What do you want?"

"I am a mischief spirit," says Lucas. "And

By the time he reached the turn into Gillygate, he was done in. As Josh stopped for an instant to catch his breath, he saw a **tall brick building** leaning over him in the moonlight. He glanced up at the inscription over the door - "**Blood and Fire**," it said. Josh looked at the blood trickling down his arm, black in the light of the torch...blood and fire...

Suddenly, Josh saw a goose waddling up the road leading back into the city. Some instinct, buried deep in his brain, made him follow... Josh walked steadily up the street, wondering what to do next.

He suddenly noticed a **torch extinguisher** on the wall of one of the houses. Josh didn't know why, but he was sure it was a sign. He plunged the torch up into the metal cylinder and waited for Spall

in the dark.

Moments later, Josh heard footsteps coming closer.

"You will come with me, boy," said a soft voice in the night.

"Never!" Josh could make him out now, a tall figure moving in the shadows.

"Light dies," murmured the voice, "darkness waits..."

The fountain spray makes him
bright green –
The grandest emperor
the world has seen.

Constantine sits on his
metal throne
Now he's no time to feel alone.
Too busy watching the
children play –
Enjoying their company
day after day.

I shivered.

"Come, if you are his blood line we have to get you out of here. There is a place. It's where Tom got out."

"What...I mean where...?"

"Ssssh, save your breath. I need to concentrate on where we are going. We

don't have Snickel now and I can't move fast."

I had so many questions, but my shoulder was hurting and I wasn't certain I really wanted to know the answers anyway. I had a chance to escape. That's all that mattered. We trudged through sewers and earth tunnels for what seemed an eternity.

ee everything you do. You're lazy, naughty, and you're mean to animals. You, Matthew Trimble, are even naughtier than me!"

"So, do I get a reward?" says Matthew, cheekily.

"No!" Lucas hisses at him, "I don't like little boys who are mean to animals. And if I see you pull your cat's tail one more time, or chase after pigeons, or kick a dog, I will turn you into a mouse and make Domino eat you! What's more, if you don't stop being so lazy and naughty all the time, I might just take a liking to haunting you forever!" Matthew stands outside the shop, shaking.

He starts to walk away, but then thinks better of it. He looks up nervously at the stone cat again and scowls. He doesn't want to find out if the strange voice is telling the truth. He decides to go and do his jobs and vows never to hurt another animal again. Not even a fly. Just in case.

So from that day on he leaves Domino in

"You can't scare me!" shouted Josh, feeling a momentary twinge of doubt.

"Light fades, darkness lives…"

The voice was low and hypnotic…the words echoed in Josh's mind. Light…. Darkness…Light. Light had to be the answer!

Josh realised that Spall was now standing beside him. Suddenly his instinct took over once again. With the last of his strength, he shoved past Spall and sprinted up Gillygate towards the City walls. There! A light was coming from the **archway**, expanding into a golden blaze that poured through into the darkness. But Spall was almost on him - inches away - he could smell his breath…

Spall's hand was on Josh's shoulder as he plunged through the archway into the light.

He knows them all and learns
from each one,
Looking on as they run in the sun.

His knees and his toes, now

worn and golden
From little hands that rub them
and hold them.

At each full moon, when
magic's around

Eventually we came to a stop. We had been wading through a clean water pipe for the last few minutes, which was a relief after the putrid stench of the sewers. Now, above us, was another pipe leading vertically upwards.

"Where are we?"

"We are under an **old well off Gillygate.**

Tom said a chant and water began miraculously to flow upwards, carrying him with it. I wasn't sure that he had survived, but years later I heard some tourists talking near a drain about a Tom Adams who put statues of cats on the buildings he designed. I think he was remembering his time down here and that the statues are in

silent thanks to Snickel, who saved his life. Anyway we have little time to waste."

"But what about you? Can't you come too?" I felt like crying again. I'd stopped seeing Mark as disgusting. He seemed to care about what happened to me.

"It's impossible for me. Rachel showed me that." His tone was heavy with despair, but

peace, even rescuing the curious cat one day when it gets stuck on the roof of the **King's Manor**. At least I think it was Domino…

Now, I know what you want to know. Did Matilda the stone cat keep the mice and rats away? Well of course not! Only real cats can do that. But the strange thing is that Domino suddenly found his hunting instinct. Of course, Liza says it was because the stone cat was good luck and had given Domino his courage back. Matthew, however, knew the stone cat was *magic*.

But you and I know that Lucas, despite his naughty nature and love of mischief, really has a good heart and just wanted Matthew to grow up to be an honest man who is kind to animals. And that's just what happened.

So, beware children, always be good, because you never know when Lucas might

Josh sneezed as first Spall's hand then the rest of his body turned to dust, his screams of frustration and disbelief echoing in Josh's ears.

"Where on earth have you been?" said Mum. "We were getting worried. What have you done to your hand?"

Josh blinked and felt the warm sun on his face. He watched as the whoosh of a

Constantine and Etty meet
near the town.
They talk of York and
children's DREAMS,
And how the world is not
as it seems…

Constantine, Emperor,
Never defeated,
All green and gold now,
Is proudly seated,
Outside the Minster,

Watching the people
Come and go
Come and go.

then he was brisk again. "Come on, the best thing you can do for me is to get out of here. You must stand under the pipe and say these words:

I'm not the one for Grim,
I'm not proper and prim.
Him I cannot make pure,

For I have sworn and cussed.
So I must now go, certain and sure,
Leaving with a gush and
an upward thrust.

"Be careful to say pure and sure so that they rhyme. Tom had to say it twice."

I was careful. Nothing happened. I tried to think as wilfully as I could and said it again. Nothing happened. I looked helplessly at Mark, my hope draining away.

"It's as I feared. You are going to have to confront him before you can go."

I suspected that there was something Mark wasn't telling me, he had seemed almost relieved when the chant hadn't worked.

be watching…

passing lorry picked up a scrap of black cloth and flung it high into the air.

He thought for a moment.

"I'm not really sure," he said truthfully. He was just glad to be back where he belonged.

He turned and watched as a goose walked up the road and disappeared from view.

But before I could challenge him, he whistled and Snickel arrived, pawed us up onto his back and we shot off down the water pipe towards Exhibition Square.

trail 2

Hello, 'tis I the Wind again! Catch up with me in the winter time. Me and the air fairies are travelling rather slowly, stirring up the air waves as we go. If I am not mistaken, here comes a familiar figure to join us.

With fire in her eyes, a shock of white hair and a silver icicle coat draped around her shoulders, it's Jaconetta Frost. Now Jaconetta has a bit of a temper, so watch out folks!

"Hello, Mr Wind. Hello, air fairies," she says icily. "What are you up to?"

"Oh, just taking the morning air, Jaconetta. It's very pleasant in the winter sun."

"Well, I'm planning a nice frost for later, for the good people of York," she hisses. "I'm in a foul mood and I'm bored with watching them *not* shivering. I even heard one fool wishing for snow! Oh, they'll get snow all right!"

"Calm down, Jaconetta," says Mirabelle, shaking her red curls. "You need a story to

"**H**ave at you, vile serf!"

Josh made a wild swing with his umbrella as though he were chopping down a tree. Fran ducked under her brother's arm and lunged, flicking the tip of her own brolly under his chin.

"Wow! You're quite good, sis!"

"Fencing Club. Thursday lunchtime."

"I despair!" said Mum, walking towards them from **King's Manor**. "I told you to wait outside the Art Gallery - and you're fencing with umbrellas! Why can't you behave like normal children?"

"I blame the parents," Josh whispered, and they both giggled.

"Your dad's going to be another couple of hours, but he'll meet us at JORVIK later on. Josh, do you still want to go to Barley Hall?"

Fran winced as Josh nodded enthusiastically. "It's dead medieval! They show you how to roast an ox! They take this long iron spike and push it..."

"Saw it last year when I went with school," said Fran. "Could I go and do a bit of window shopping and meet up with you later?"

Flap the Bat is scared of the dark.
Flap the Bat won't leave the park.
He won't play with his
sisters and brothers.
He feels so different from
all the others.

As we left Exhibition Square, Snickel flew down the pipe. I swallowed as I felt the icy cold that always preceded Grim on my back. He was gaining on us again. I glanced sideways and saw that the shadows around me seemed to be rearing up, ready to strike. Suddenly, Grim's slime-infested arm was wrapping itself around my neck. Fear gripped me as I grabbed onto Mark to stop myself falling. For a moment I could do nothing but watch in horror as Grim's hold tightened.

I had to free myself or I was going to be dragged off Snickel's back with or without Mark. My fingers dug into the slimy mould of Grim's arm. I thought I was going to be sick as it clogged under my fingernails. I tried to yank the arm from around my neck, but it didn't budge. I felt desperate. Then I knew what I had to do. Screwing up my nose against the cabbage smell, I bit down hard into the disgusting gunk, willing myself not to puke. I heard a roar of anger from behind me and suddenly I was free.

soothe you."

Now, Jaconetta and I always have a bet that in winter, if we can tell her a story that brings a tear to her eye and melts her frosty heart, she won't send the big freeze until late January.

If we fail, she sends it in early December.

Mum nodded reluctantly, glancing at the sky. "OK - take your brolly. It doesn't look too promising." They agreed to meet at St Mary's on Castlegate later on.

Fran wandered along St Leonard's Place, enjoying her freedom. As she walked, she glanced at the building opposite. The **Theatre Royal**. It was an odd building. The new bit looked...well...new, but the old bit looked more like a church, with all those

Flap the Bat likes warm sunlight
But ghosts and monsters
roam at night.
He hates the shadows,
so he won't go out,
What if witches on broomsticks
are whizzing about?

He hangs in his tree near the library.
The glow-worms keep him company.
He wraps himself up in
his shiny wings
And thinks of sunlight
and daytime things.

We shot forward. Snickel swung to the left into a narrow tunnel, surely too small for Grim, and then we were in a huge room.

I let go of Mark and we both slid off. My insides were churning. I could taste bits of Grim's foul flesh in my mouth. The final straw was looking down and coming eye to eye socket with a grotesquely grinning

This year we'll just see who wins...

"Are you ready for your story, Jaconetta?"

"Oh, I suppose so," she says with a bored expression.

Well - this is the tale.

Many centuries ago, the city of York was an even stranger and more magical place... Let me take you there.

One afternoon, a young man called Walter Turnpike sits on the **Roman wall** by **King's Manor**, kicking at the moss and wondering what he is ever going to do. He has two problems. The first is how to pay off his debts and the second is how to find a new job, since he has been sacked as the local town crier, on account of the fact that he is too quiet.

Walter is wondering how he is going to break the news to his wife and children, that he still hasn't found any new

pinnacles and knobbly bits.

As a shaft of sunlight moved across the building, Fran's eyes were drawn to the carved figures that decorated the front of the theatre. One figure stood out from the rest. He had a strong face, with high cheekbones and a mass of shoulder-length hair. He looked almost real...

As she stared at him, he appeared to turn

Flap wants to change because
Flap can see
This is not the way for
a bat to be.
Only when the sun begins to rise
Can Flap relax and close his eyes.

Dusk falls one day –
Flap wakes to find
He's the only bat left behind.
The other bats have flown away
Not asking if he'll go or stay!

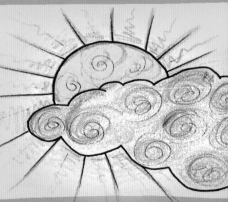

skull. I threw up all the chocolate cake from Betty's Tea Rooms. All over Mark. He didn't seem to notice.

"Where are we?" I choked as the last of the vomit cleared my tonsils.

"In the **crypt of the Theatre Royal.**" I was now as green as some of the half-dead bits of Mark as I looked around at the creepy tombs.

work, when two of his daughters come bursting over the grass behind him.

"Daddy, daddy," shouts Molly, a black-haired girl of ten, and Griselda, a girl of eight, with a mop of brown hair, follows close behind. Both of them have smudged faces and dirt on their smocks.

"What have you two been up to?" asks their father.

"We've been playing hide-and-seek outside the abbey," says Molly.

"But one of the monks saw us and chased us away," says Griselda.

his head and look her straight in the eye.

That was when it all started. Fran felt suddenly hot and sticky, and a little bit sick. She backed away, glancing round to see if anyone else had seen. No one was looking. As she walked down Museum Street, she paused at the drinking **fountain** outside the **Gardens** and cupped her hand into the water. It was icy cold. She shivered - she felt very strange.

Fran looked up. Piles of grey clouds filled the sky; the air shook gently with distant thunder. She had a funny feeling - half fear, half excitement - that something was going to happen. A harsh cry came from above, and a pair of geese flew low overhead, their wingbeats stirring the thick air. The geese cried again and circled above her. Fran was sure they were calling to her. She followed

them down to the river and found herself on **Lendal Bridge**.

The river rolled beneath her in a ribbon of black water. "It never stops," thought Fran, leaning over the railings. "The bit of river I was looking at a moment ago has gone forever. I suppose the 'me' who was looking at it has gone forever as well…"

Then the *something* that Fran had been half

Suddenly, a throaty whisper, like rough sandpaper across old wood, echoed into the chamber. Grim. I shivered.

"Come to me, Sarah. You're running out of time. You need not fear. I need you alive. You're the one I've been waiting for. You are of me. You are the Purecust who will make me complete."

"How does he know my name?" I asked Mark.

"He senses it. He was a Purecust once and he…"

"Why listen to him," came Grim's rasping voice. "Don't you realise? It's his job to deliver you to me. He's been waiting a hundred years to do it. Tell her Mark. Tell

Sarah how I need to devour her. Tell Sarah why you want her to sacrifice herself to me."

I turned and stared at Mark. I saw it in his one good eye. Grim was speaking the truth.

"Didn't you realise, Sarah, that he saved you from the rat for me? Did you not notice that Mark only decided to see if he could get you out when I let slip that you were of my

"Daddy," says Molly. "Can we go see the execution tomorrow? Old Ned is being hung for thieving and not paying his bills."

Walter shudders at the thought, looking very uncomfortable. The air fairies gasp. "Children of today!" they say.

"I don't think that's a good idea, Moll."

"Why not? Mother said we could go if we were good."

"Well," says her father, "I don't think that' a suitable thing for my daughters. Anyway children, your daddy has been looking for new job today." He thinks he had bette change the subject.

expecting - happened. A dazzling tree of light, bright beyond belief, sent its roots down from the sky, enclosing the whole city in a brilliant web. The black river gleamed like a sheet of polished metal and then, incredibly, Fran saw it slow to a stop...then move backwards!

Thunder exploded across the city, an enormous crash that rebounded from one horizon to the other. Suddenly lightning hit

the bridge and Fran screamed as she was thrown into the air. She landed with a thud on the ground.

When she opened her eyes, everything had changed. The bridge had gone for a start, and where had all the horses come from? The people looked somehow different too. As she sat up, she realised the air stank of horse muck and smoke - and fear.

As Fran got up to ask someone what wa going on, she nearly fell over her own feet Her jeans and t-shirt had been replaced with a huge skirt and woollen cape.

A man wearing long riding boots and a leather jerkin was walking slowly toward her. Fran stepped forward, carefully lifting her skirts with one hand.

"Excuse me, sir," she said, "but can you tel

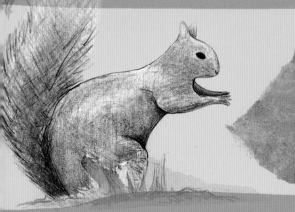

blood?"

"No, please, it can't be," I begged, turning again to Mark.

"It's not that simple, Sarah," said Mark in a trembling voice that turned my stomach. "Let me explain."

"No-o-o-o," I screamed. A dangerous laugh

from Grim echoed round the chamber. Mark began to walk towards me. The good part of his face was pleading and caring, but it was just a front. I was being backed towards the tunnel where Grim was waiting to grab me. Suddenly, Snickel shot out a paw, lifted me up and tossed me out of Grim's reach. I spotted a crack in the wall of the crypt just

ahead of me and raced through.

The tunnel I was in was too small for Snickel and Mark couldn't move that fast on his decaying limbs. I was now all alone. I ran blindly ahead, but was brought nearly to a stop as I became tangled in some bindweed that hung from the tunnel roof, sticking to my clothes.

Distant scraping sounds. Probably Mark

he girls jump up and down for joy, as the ir fairies circle around them, curiously ulling at their long hair. "Daddy's got a ob!" shouts Griselda. "What is it?"

"Well I – " Walter looks embarrassed. I look ight through him as he searches the air for an answer. "I'm a - unicorn catcher," he says. "By royal appointment!"

"A unicorn catcher!" The girls are amazed.

"But don't tell your mother yet," says Walter. "It's a surprise."

Mirabelle is shocked. "Lying to your children," she says. "You can't keep it a secret forever."

"Never mind, Mirabelle," I say, ruffling at Walter's slightly shabby clothes. "He'll think of something."

Just then, we see a tubby little man approaching. He has a wave of dark hair and a lopsided walk.

"Well, look who it is - Rufus Borwick!" says

---

me what's happening?"

The man looked at her in bewilderment.

"Where have you been, girl? York is taken by the Roundhead army, and King Charles's men must go to **St Helen's Square** to be disarmed." As he moved off, Fran stared at his back, her thoughts a whirlwind of confusion. Roundhead? King Charles? Suddenly it dawned on her. Reason

---

Flap squeaks with panic
and starts to shiver!
Flap sets the treetops all a-quiver.
He asks a squirrel skipping by,
"Where've the bats all gone,
and why?"

"They've moved on
now that winter's here.
The winds grow cold
this time of year.
It's a very long way to go,
young Flap,
But I can help - I'll draw a map."

The squirrel scratches in the ground
As the darkness falls all around.
Brave Flap finally leaves his perch
To go in search of
St Michael's Church.

---

coming after me. I tried to speed up again, but the ground was stony and I kept stumbling. Suddenly, as I rounded a bend, there was a drop in front of me that seemed to go on forever. It was like a ski jump and much too steep and smooth to try to clamber down.

Ski jump. Yes! I had learned to snowboard last winter and looked around frantically. I

Walter. Rufus is the nightwatchman who lives in **Barker Tower**.

"What are you doing here, Walter - why aren't you out towncrying?" says Rufus with a grin.

"Daddy's not a town crier any more," pipes up Molly, glaring at him.

"No - he's a unicorn catcher!" says Griselda.

"Oh," says Rufus looking at them and then at their father who just shrugs.

We hear Molly whisper to her sister,"I don't like him. His eyes are too close together!"

"She's right!" says Mirabelle to me. The air

fairies mumble amongst themselves sensing Walter is about to be led astray.

"Well now, Mr - Unicorn Catcher," says Rufus. "Why don't you join me and the boys in a little game of cards? Being as you got time on your hands and all. Give you a chance to win some money - in your hour of

screamed at her that this could not be happening - she must have hit her head or something. But her eyes told her she was still in York, but York of the 17th century, right in the middle of the Civil War.

"This isn't happening," Fran thought. "Time can't go backwards!" Fran looked round frantically, searching for some clue. Her

Flap waggles along on shaky wings
And thinks of sunlight
and daytime things.
Flap forgets the map, skips a turn.
Flap still has so much to learn!

Flap flies low above dark water.
Flap goes further than he ought to.
Soon, he doesn't know
where he is…
He swoops and hangs under
the bridge.

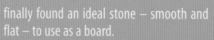

finally found an ideal stone – smooth and flat – to use as a board.

Through the silence came the sound of panting. Mark. He was close.

"Sarah. Stop. You don't understand!"

I was not going to be fooled by his pleading. I pulled strands of bindweed off me and

strapped my feet to the stone. Mark sounded very close now. I looked down at the drop in front of me, took a deep breath and slid forward.

I almost fell off in the first few seconds as the stone accelerated over the loose earth. I tried to turn in order to slow down, but the edge of the stone didn't work like a

eed." He gives a sly wink.

Why not," says Walter eagerly. So off they
o, with us following, to the alehouse.

olly and Griselda sit by the window and
atch as their daddy gambles away all his
oney, then his flute, then his coat. Rufus
huckles at every loss, seeming to get

bigger and greedier by the minute.

Molly nudges Griselda. "Daddy's losing
everything to that horrid man! We should
do something."

Just then - "Look!" cries Griselda, as a streak
of white brightness passes in the sky
overhead. The girls look up in amazement.

eyes fell on the river. "It's impossible! You
can't see the same river twice!"

ran had never felt so alone. She thought of
Mum and Josh and her bedroom at home,
and the more she thought of them, the
more they seemed to fade away into an
infinite distance. "What am I going to do?"
She could feel tears welling up in her eyes.
"Get a grip," she thought, swallowing hard.
"I can't just stand here. Someone will

notice." She joined the flow of people along
Lendal and into **St Helen's Square**.

It was packed with people and horses. A
troop of Parliament cavalry was in front of
the church. They were big men on big
horses; each had a sword in his hand.
The leader's horse was smaller than the
rest. He sat straight in the saddle, a tall
bearded man with a scarlet sash over his

shoulder. He glanced round the square,
then reached into his saddlebag and took
out a piece of paper.

"Who's that?" Fran whispered to the woman
standing next to her.

"Sir Thomas Fairfax," she said. "One of their
best generals. He was the one who won the
battle for them yesterday."

snowboard in snow. I just managed to
steady myself and headed straight down,
faster and faster, into the darkness. Then
suddenly from behind me came a high-
pitched wail.

"Sarah, NO. NO-O-O."

The piercing desperation of the scream
made me turn my head. Mark was

silhouetted in all his disgusting glory at the
top of the slope, arms – or what was left of
them – outstretched.

Turning was a big mistake. I felt the stone
slip beneath me; then I was falling. Hard.
Luckily, after just a few feet, the slope
flattened off.

I came to a stop, bruised all over. My

"It's a unicorn, Moll! A real unicorn!"

Mirabelle and some of the air fairies are riding on her back, though the children can't see *them*.

"Come on!" cries Molly and the two race out of the door to chase the unicorn.

On and on the white streak travels, like a powerful horse but with huge feather wings, beating the clouds out of its path towards the evening sky. The air fairies are painting the sky in the shades of dusk mauve, lilac and a glow of orange. Further and further, the girls give chase, until at last they come to a forest where they have never been before.

A drum rolled somewhere and the crowd stilled.

"Citizens of York!" The leader's voice had an air of easy authority. It was the voice of a man used to being obeyed. "The army of Charles Stuart, so-called King of England, has been defeated. This city belongs to Parliament."

He paused, letting the news sink in.

"I have here a list of all those officers who served on the Royalist side. I ask you now to step forward when I call out your name and surrender your weapons. You will then be taken to London for further interrogation." His mouth smiled, but his eyes stayed cold and determined. "Any attempt to escape will be treated with the utmost severity." Fairfax raised his arm, and musket barrels appeared at every window, pointing down into the square. Looking round, Fran could see that every exit was blocked by a line of Parliament soldiers.

"Captain Thomas Adams!"

A small, plump man carrying two enormous pistols stepped uncertainly forward. He was relieved of his weapons and pushed to one side.

"Major William Blake!"

shoulder was bleeding where the rat's claws had dug in. I didn't want to move, but I probably had less than two hours and no one to help me now. From around a corner ahead, I could hear water gently lapping over stones. I edged forward on hands and knees and looked up.

Tears came to my eyes.

Ahead of me was a beautiful lake. It was such a shock to find something like this amongst all the horror under the ground. There were different shades of red, orange, yellow, green and blue light shimmering in turn across the water. The cavern's roof was dark, with odd specks of silver-white rock showing through like stars.

I knelt there for several precious minutes before my dulled thoughts were sharpened by the now-familiar drop in temperature and shifting, menacing shadows that meant Grim was nearby. I looked around, dread knotting in my stomach. On the opposite shore of the lake was an opening in the rock near some ancient-looking

Out of breath, Molly gasps, "Where did it go?"

'Look," whispers her sister, pulling her sleeve. There, between the two tallest trees, is the most beautiful creature they have ever seen, drinking from a stream. The unicorn tosses her mane and stamps her feet, as the girls dare to go a bit closer, but still keep hidden.

Just then, they notice a man emerge from the undergrowth, carrying a large net and tiptoeing ever so silently up to the unicorn. They know him. It's Merrick, York's very own street entertainer. He stands on the corner and recites verse, sometimes he'll juggle or play out of tune music on a lute.

"No!" cry the air fairies as one voice.

"No!" cry the children, running out of their hiding place. But I, the Wind, know what intelligent creatures unicorns are. The unicorn has already sensed she is not alone and, quick as a wink, she flies up into the

A kind of queue was forming along one side of the square. Some were dressed in rich brocade, stained with mud and filth, others still wearing breastplates and leg armour - all of them with the helpless look of a defeated army. Those York men who had fought for the King were surrounded by their families, weeping and hugging and giving them parcels of food for their uncertain journey.

It's the darkest place he's ever been.
He feels sick. His face turns green.
Creepy noises, webs on his face,
He flaps fast from that place.

Swooping up out the other side,
Flap sees an angel with wings
spread wide.

He watches the boats sail
safely under.
Flap looks on with fear and wonder.

City lights reflect in the river,
Which make Flap
feel slightly better.

stones. I watched as Grim half walked, half slid through the opening, his disgusting body heaving with the effort.

"Welcome," came the throaty whisper.

I tried to look confident – wilful.

"You don't fool me, young Purecust." That horrible, dry, evil laugh. "But you shouldn't be scared of me. We need each other. It is fortunate that you have come to *my* lake. When they put the pumping station into the old **Lendal Tower**, what, about 150 years ago now, they didn't realise what they would create for me."

Grim began to edge round the lake towards me. I started to shuffle on my knees the

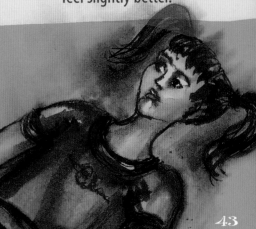

air, just as Merrick is about to throw his net over her, and lands in a tree. The unicorn looks down from the tree and gives a mocking little neigh, throwing back her head. She seems to be laughing at Merrick and the air fairies all join in, clapping and cheering.

"You can't catch a unicorn," shouts Mirabelle. Not that anyone can hear her.

"Well, thanks a bunch, you pair of scamps," says Merrick, turning on the two girls.

"You were going to kill it!" says Molly indignantly.

Fran wandered aimlessly through the crowd. It was better to keep moving, she thought. Maybe, when the soldiers had gone, she might find a way back...

"Pardon me," said a voice behind her, "but...I seem to know you..." He was young – no more than fifteen – and although his face was filthy and he had a black eye, she recognised him at once. It was his face she had seen on the front of the **Theatre Royal**.

"I think...I think I've seen you before as well," said Fran, her heart pounding in her chest.

"Alexander Gribham," he said, "My friends call me Sandy." He looked down shyly at the ground, "You were in my dream last night."

"Oh," Fran held out her hand. "Frances Marchant," she said. "You can call me Fran."

Sandy wiped the back of his hand across his face. "My father was killed yesterday." Fran didn't know what to say. "He wasn't a lord or a knight or anything. He was a farmer. He was just doing what he thought was right...They'll take our land," said Sandy quietly. "They'll take everything...unless... In my dream, you said you'd help me," he finished quickly.

other way, towards a shadow that I hoped was another opening from this cave.

"Not planning to leave me, are you?" Then the whisper turned from taunt to command, "Look into the lake. There's something I can only show you through water."

In the lake, a black circle of glass-smooth water formed. Slowly, pictures began to appear. I forgot about moving round the lake and began to watch closely, desperately hoping this would help me make some sense of what was happening.

The pictures started with a young boy who was obviously poor and lived a long time ago. The boy got older. He worked in the

No I wasn't, Molly, you've got it all wrong," says Merrick. "I just wanted a unicorn as a pet."

The unicorn is free," says Griselda. "It can't be a pet."

Anyway, our dad's a unicorn catcher," says Molly. "It's *his* job." She looks embarrassed.

Now that she has seen how beautiful the unicorn is, it suddenly doesn't seem a job to be proud of any more.

Merrick throws back his head and laughs.

"Your dad is no such thing!" he says. "He's probably never seen a unicorn in his life." The unicorn snorts from her safe place in the tree.

"Maybe daddy wasn't telling the truth," says Molly thoughtfully. "He's in the tavern now gambling all his money away. Maybe he just made it up."

"More than likely," says Merrick, settling down on the grass, the bells on his cap making a gentle tinkling sound as he takes it off. "I thought it would be good to bring

ran saw a glimmer of hope in his grey eyes.

My father's sword. He gave it to me esterday, before the battle...just in ase..."

andy was wearing it on a belt slung over his shoulder. The hand guard was polished teel in the shape of a flying goose, with wo tiny green jewels for eyes.

Flap thinks more clearly
and turns around.
Then weakly flaps back into town.

Flap flies down **Lendal**
towards the Square,
To a church with
coloured windows there.

In the darkness is many a light
Shining steadily in the night.

St Helen watches all the while
And greets young Flap with a smile.
"Little traveller, you are so bold
Flying all alone in the cold."

Flap squeaks and peeps
through shaking wings
And thinks of sunlight
and daytime things.
A ghost! Flap feels too young to die.
Flap bites his lip.
Flap starts to cry.

fields and then seemed to live in a small room with lots of others. People shouted at him a lot. He was hit quite a bit, first by older people and then, as he grew, by others in fights. His face became scarred and ugly.

Then it all went blank. I looked up and realised that Grim had slithered closer to

me. Maybe this was all a trick. I was about to move when the pictures started again. I couldn't help but watch. I *had* to understand what was going on.

An old man in a cloak with a white beard, on top of a bonfire. Then, flames rose, slowly reaching higher and he burned into a pile of ash. The ash was gathered up and

put into a golden box. As the lid went down over the ash, I saw two letters dripped in silver on it: GF. The pictures faded away again.

I sensed a further drop in temperature. Grim was much closer. I started to move this time. But there were still more pictures.

Another young boy. This time the soft face of someone you knew was spoiled. The boy

the unicorn into York, as part of my act, but then I'd have a lot of alchemists after me."

"What's an alchemist?" asks Griselda.

"It's someone who turns metal into gold," says Merrick. "Some of them are proper wizards, but some of them are liars. Some bad alchemists claim that the horn of the unicorn is useful in magic, you see, and

then they hunt for them. They would kill them! Rufus Borwick - he claims to be an alchemist, but he's just a con man. He's the type."

"Rufus Borwick - that's who daddy's losing money to!" says Molly.

"Well," Merrick shakes his head. "You

"It's Spanish," said Sandy. "From Toledo. They're the best. It belonged to my grandfather. He was a smuggler of secrets," he added proudly. He slid the blade a couple of inches out of the scabbard.

Fran had never seen anything so beautiful, or so deadly.

"If only I could get it to Jamie..." Sandy was whispering now. "There is information hidden in the hilt...information that can save my family, give my mother and sisters a second chance..."

"Who's Jamie?"

"My younger brother. He wasn't at the battle. Now my father's dead and I'm a captive, he's our only hope."

"Where is he?"

"I made him stay at Tom Campion's...it's a

coffee house down there...the one with the **Coat of Arms** above the door." He nodded towards **Davygate**, past the line of soldiers. "They're all loyal King's men..."

Something told Fran this was important. The geese flying towards the bridge, the goose on the sword... "I'll do it. I'll find your brother and give him the sword."

She realised what she had said. Her scalp

grew older through scenes of lavish meals and servants in uniform. Then the pictures of him began to change. He was more secretive-looking, his eyes darting around, looking for danger. I saw flashes of York. The city walls. The young man was often in dark places. Suddenly, there was an explosion and he was running from stones collapsing

around him. More secretive-looking meetings. More underground explosions. Just before the water went black again, a close up of the man. A gold locket hung round his neck with GF picked out in silver.

So, I had seen an old white-bearded man burned and his ashes being carried in a locket round the neck of a rich man who

was secretly blowing things up around York. I wondered where the poor ugly man with the scars fitted into all of this and how it had anything to do with me?

"Are you confused?" came the grating whisper. "The last piece of the story should help."

The water started to change again. But I

daddy's in trouble then."

The girls look downcast at this. The unicorn cautiously edges down from the tree. She knows that something has changed and that she can trust the humans now.

She sits by the girls while they stroke and plait her mane. Merrick sings a song, out of tune, and the air fairies smile to each other as if this is the most pretty music they have ever heard. Then the unicorn stands up, shakes her mane at the girls, and looks at them as if she wants them to follow her. She trots away into a clearing. The girls follow and she stops, looking down on the ground and pawing at it with her hoof. There they see a glistening gold key, with a ruby at the centre. Molly pounces on it.

"It's a gift from the unicorn!" she exclaims. "Look, Merrick."

"That's a rare and precious thing," says Merrick, looking at the key. "Don't you

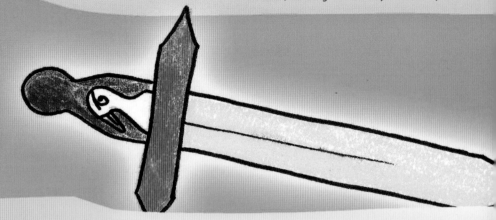

crawled with terror. Then came another feeling - a feeling of certainty. This was why she was here, why the river had run backwards and carried her with it.

"Give me a hug," she said, "as though I'm your sister."

As he took her in his arms, Fran slid the sword from Sandy's shoulders and hid it under her cloak. "Good luck, Sandy," she

"B…B…Beautiful lady,
I need to find
The way to St Michael's,
if you don't mind.
The other bats have left me alone.
I'm scared of the dark,"
Flap adds with a groan.

Says St Helen, "You're going
the right way.
You'll be there, I promise,
for break of day.
But listen well before you go,
All alone? It isn't so!

was not going to be fooled. It *was* a trap. Grim was getting too close. I sprang up and sprinted round the lake towards the opening I had seen earlier. I realised it was big enough for Grim to squeeze through too. But I didn't have a choice. I couldn't go back.

It was pitch black. I ran as fast as I dared,

know what this is, Molly? It's the key to happiness."

"What does it do?" says Griselda.

"Well," says Merrick. "There's an old legend that says if the unicorn favours you - and I guess she likes you two a lot - you will find the key to happiness.

This key will unlock a box somewhere and in that box, well there could be anything treasure, magic, whatever you think will make us happy."

"If we can find the box then there might be enough money in it to make us rich!" says Molly excitedly.

"Let's give it to daddy!" says Griselda. "It's getting dark now."

"Well, maybe if you ask the unicorn nicely she'll take you home," says Merrick.

"Farewell little beauty," says Merrick to the unicorn. "Watch out for Rufus, girls," he says to them, as they set off on their

whispered. He smiled sadly.

The soldiers at the checkpoint on **Davygate** didn't give her a second glance - just another Royalist brat weeping for her brother. Fran's tears were real enough - the first grown-up tears she had shed. What was going to happen to him? She only looked back once. Sandy was climbing into a cart with the other prisoners. He was careful not to look in her direction.

My name in Greek
means *candlelight*,
In darkness burning true and bright.
When you're afraid, Flap
think of me
And a light in the dark
you will see."

He thanks Helen and flaps onward
Flapping higher now and upward.
Then suddenly, Flap lets out a howl
As he crashes head first
into an **owl**!

The owl drops the spider
he's been eating
And keeps on going,
huge wings beating.

Flap squeaks and crashes to the
ground.

slipping on the mud — it must be close to the river. I turned a corner and fell through a hole in a brick wall. Tumbling to my feet, I found myself in a huge cellar. Giant wooden beer barrels stamped with **Lendal** Cellars were scattered around.

I heard Grim coming through behind me. In a blind panic, I rushed up the sloping floor

Trail 2 – EXHIBITION SQUARE to ST MARY'S CASTLEGATE

21 Roman Wall *in the car park next to the council building on St Leonard's Place*

22 Theatre Royal *on St Leonard's Place (opposite side of the road)*

23 Crypt under Theatre Royal *not visible from the outside*

24 Water fountain outside Museum Gardens *on Museum Street, set into the wall on your right, before you reach the gates of the Museum Gardens, when walking towards Lendal Bridge*

25 St Mary's Abbey/Museum Gardens *the Museum Gardens are accessible through a set of gates on Museum Street. The abbey is at the back of the gardens; both are open to the public during daylight hours*

26 Lendal Tower (Water Tower) *Lendal Tower is the tower to your right as you approach Lendal Bridge*

27 Lendal Bridge

28 Barker Tower *Barker Tower is to your right at the end of Lendal Bridge. Cross over the road at the end of the bridge, using the two pedestrian crossings, and walk back up the other side of the bridge*

29 Lendal *turn right into Lendal off Museum Street, opposite the entrance to the Museum Gardens*

30 St Helen's Square *square at the end of Lendal*

31 St Helen's Church *church in St Helen's Square, next to the bottom of Stonegate*

32 Davygate *when facing St Helen's Church, turn right down Davygate*

33 Coat of arms *on no. 1 New Street (corner of Davygate)*

34 Owl mosaic *with St Helen's Square behind you, find the recessed area with gravestones on Davygate (right hand side) and then look up at the wall to your left*

35 St Sampson's Square *square at the end of Davygate*

36 Feasegate *at the end of St Sampson's Square, before walking into Parliament Street, turn right into Feasegate, right again into Market Street and then left into Spurriergate*

37 St Michael's Church *when on Spurriergate, look right for the Spurriergate Centre, on the corner with Low Ousegate. This is St Michael's Church*

38 Nessgate *at the end of Spurriergate, walk straight on WITHOUT crossing the road, into Nessgate. Continue straight on, over pelican crossing, into Castlegate*

Trail 3 – ST MARY'S CASTLEGATE to THE MINSTER

39 St Mary's Church, Castlegate *church is to your left, set back from the road. Starting point of Trail 3*

40 Castlegate House *walk up Castlegate. Castlegate House is to your right, on the other side of the road*

41 Clifford's Tower *at the end of Castlegate, look straight ahead. Follow the footpath round the corner, without crossing any roads; this will take you into the Coppergate Centre*

42 Fairfax House *tall building to your left. Keep walking until you pass St Mary's again on your left*

43 JORVIK *past St Mary's, JORVIK is to your left*

44 Lantern Tower (All Saints, Pavement) *walk up through the Coppergate Centre; at the top ahead of you is All Saints, Pavement, on the other side of the road*

45 & 46 Merchant Adventurers' Hall & Gate *turn right out of the Coppergate Centre until you reach Pavement and cross over the road using the pedestrian crossing. Turn right down Pavement and the hall is to your left, set back and down from the road*

47 Foss Bridge *walk down past the hall, turn left without crossing the road, follow the road round and cross over the river using Foss Bridge*

48 St Crux Parish Hall *walk up to the top of Fossgate, cross the road carefully and ahead of you is St Crux Church Hall, next to Whip-ma-whop-ma-gate*

49 Shambles *turn right into the Shambles*

50 King's Square *square at the top of the Shambles*

51 Tom Adams's Cat *as you come out of the Shambles, walk into the square and turn around so that the Shambles is to your right. Look up at the rooftops in front of you*

52 Eadwig Pig *at the end of King's Square, turn left down Church Street and then first right down Swinegate. Towards the bottom of Swinegate, opposite Back Swinegate, turn right into Swinegate Court East, and take the first left. The statue is on the wall to your right. Go back to Swinegate the way you came*

53 Letters on bricks of York Central Mission Hall *after exiting Swinegate Court East, cross straight over Swinegate into Back Swinegate The York Central Mission is on the corner with Swinegate, to your left*

54 Stonegate *follow the road round to the right into Little Stonegate. At the end turn right into Stonegate*

55 Red devil *on the wall on the right hand side, by Coffee Yard*

56 Minerva *above the shop on the corner, diagonally to your left, at the entrance to Minster Gates*

57 Minster Gates *cross over High Petergate into Minster Gates, with the Minster in front of you*

ormation

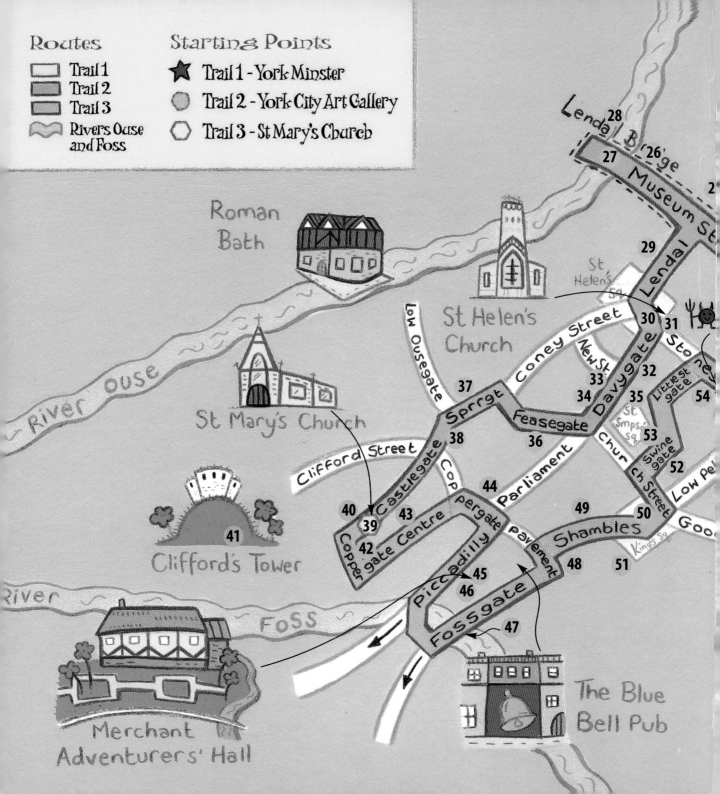

Numbers 1-57 – points of interest (please see overleaf)

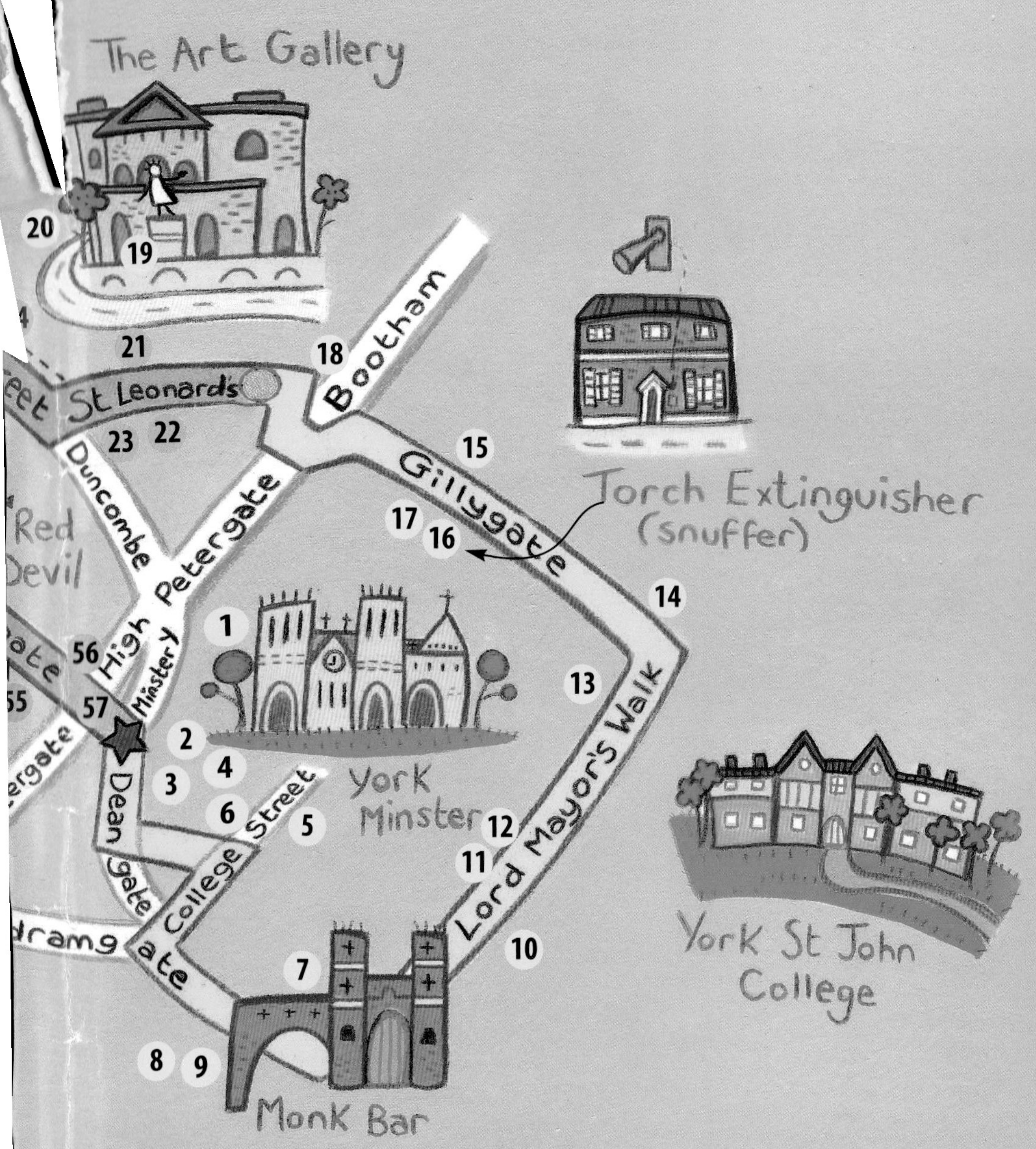

The Art Gallery

20
19
21

St Leonards
23 22

Bootham

15
Gillygate

Torch Extinguisher
(snuffer)

18

Duncombe

Red
Devil

High Petergate

Minster Y

17 16

14

1

13

56
57

2
3   4
6
5

College Street

York
Minster

Lord Mayor's Walk

12
11

10

York St John
College

Dean gate

dram g ate

7

8   9

Monk Bar

York
Breadcrumbs

Trail 1 – The MINSTER to EXHIBITION SQUARE

1. **The Minster** *starting point of Trail 1*

2. **Statue of Constantine the Great** *near the South door of the Minster*

3. **Roman Column** *across the path from the statue of Constantine*

4. **The Queen's Path** *runs from Constantine to College Green*

5. **St William's College** *next to the Minster, on College Green*

6. **Sundial on College Green** *opposite St William's College*

7. **Elbow Lane (Monk Bar Court)** *left off Goodramgate, immediately before Monk Bar*

8. **Monk Bar** *gateway at the end of Goodramgate*

9. **Wild men of Monk Bar** *on the outside of Monk Bar at the very top of the battlements*

10. **Groves Lane/Roman road** *when walking up Lord Mayor's Walk, look to your right (across the road) for a small alleyway between numbers 22A and 24; this is Groves Lane*

11. **Lord Mayor's Walk** *road that runs adjacent to the city walls*

12. **Moat** *stretch of grass that runs along Lord Mayor's Walk, beneath the city walls*

13. **City walls/Robin Hood's Tower** *Robin Hood's Tower is the tower at the end of the stretch of city walls that run adjacent to Lord Mayor's Walk*

14. **Salvation Army building** *as you turn left into Gillygate from Lord Mayor's Walk, cross the road at the pedestrian crossing. The Salvation Army building is in front of you*

15. **Gillygate (and the well)**

16. **Torch snuffer/extinguisher** *is to the left of the door of no. 28 Gillygate (opposite side of the road)*

17. **White cat** *the white cat sits above the window of no. 26 Gillygate (opposite side of the road)*

18. **Stone arch** *at the top of Gillygate, cross the road at the pedestrian crossing and walk under the stone arch (through to Exhibition Square and the Art Gallery)*

19. **William Etty** *statue outside the Art Gallery*

20. **King's Manor** *to your left when facing the Art Gallery*

York Breadcrumbs
Points of interest & inf

ourney back to the city. He decides to ollow on foot.

Even I have trouble keeping up with that unicorn - she's a fast creature! In a twinkling, skimming over the long stone city walls, the girls are back outside the tavern. Once inside, they are dismayed to find that their father hasn't won a penny back and instead has now lost his pig and his best hat! I shake my wavy head at the air fairies as we watch through the window, and they sigh at Walter's stupidity.

"Where have you two been?" exclaims their father.

Tom Campion's Coffee House was packed tight as a barrel of herrings. People were crammed on benches round a long table, drinking from brown pottery mugs, shouting to each other across the room. A bright fire burned in the grate and above it hung a polished copper boiler for the coffee. Enthroned in an armchair by the fire was a huge, broad-shouldered man with a gleaming bald head. He was poking the fire with an old dagger.

Fran pulled the cloak round her shoulders and stepped inside. The place smelled of sweat and tobacco smoke and coffee. It was difficult for Fran to make her way through the press with the sword hidden under her cloak. She prodded one man in the back, but he swore at the man next to him and never even saw her.

At last she reached the fire. The big man looked up and smiled.

"What can I do for you, love?"

"I'm...looking for someone..."

"You'll have a job finding anyone today. York's all topsy-turvy with the Parliament coming in. Do I know this person you're looking for?"

"Are you Tom Campion?"

towards an enormous door. Halfway across the floor, I began to feel strange. My head felt woozy. Everything began to go out of focus. My legs suddenly collapsed under me. As I hit the ground, my vision came back. What was happening? Then it struck me. The ground was sloping upwards. I knew then that I couldn't go above ground level or something dreadful would happen. I felt fear deep in my gut. I couldn't escape from Grim. But worse, I could never go above ground again anyway. I had never felt so completely alone.

"I feel that you have seen sense, young Purecust," he whispered. "No point in fighting me, is there?" He slithered towards me and stopped a few feet from where I was lying. I braced myself. Would he eat me, or would he just sort of ooze over me? His arm shot out and I thought my heart was going to stop. "Please don't let this be happening to me," I sobbed silently. But his arm didn't reach me. Instead, it knocked over one of the barrels which splintered and

"We found a real unicorn!" says Griselda.

"And she gave us a key," says Molly. "Look - if you open the box with this, it'll be full of money, daddy."

Through the window, I notice Rufus slavering at the thought of more riches.

"There's no such things as unicorns," say Walter.

"There is," insists Molly.

"You told us there were," says Griselda.

Walter hangs his head.

"Well, that was a little white lie, girls.

He nodded.

"I'm looking for Jamie Gribham."

Tom Campion's face took on a guarded, cautious look.

"Have you seen him?"

"He was here."

"Was?"

"He went out an hour since...looking for

work, or so he said. He'll be back any minute, I expect..."

He smiled again, though it was somehow different this time. "You could always wait upstairs if you wanted," he said. "Maybe you'd like a cup of hot chocolate...on the house."

Fran suddenly felt very tired. "Thanks," she said, "I'd like that."

"You just go up them stairs," urged Tom, "and I'll bring you the chocolate up in a couple of minutes."

Fran sat by the window, looking down into the crowded street. She felt a surge of panic. "What if Jamie doesn't come back?" she thought. "I don't even know what he looks like. And if I can't give him the wretched sword..." Fran was sure that the sword was the key. If she didn't complete

beer poured out and settled into puddles.

"You haven't seen the last episode of my story yet. Look into the pool at your feet."

Images began to form. The poor, ugly boy, now a young man, was in uniform, standing proudly in front of York Minster. A series of scenes with him secretly following the rich man who had the GF locket around

his neck. They were in dark passageways and rooms, one of them this very cellar I was in now. In one or two places the rich man set off explosions. The pictures stopped and the pool went black for a few moments. Then a bright room. The two young men faced each other.

The rich one pulled out a knife. The poor

one pulled out a whistle. Before the whistle could be blown, the rich one attacked. The knife knocked the whistle out of the poor one's hand and sliced into his uniform. He tried to grab the knife, but missed and caught the locket's chain instead. The locket sprung open and the ashes flew out. The ashes briefly formed into the old white-

'm not really a unicorn catcher. That's why 'm trying to win some money here off Rufus."

Griselda bites her lip and looks at her sister who whispers, "Told you!"

"Where did you see this unicorn, girls?" says Rufus.

Molly shakes her head. "Not telling," she says.

Just then, Merrick walks in. "Evening Rufus," he says.

"This key looks worth a bit of money," says Walter, turning it over in his hands.

"If it's true what these little tykes say," says Rufus, "you find that box and it'll make your fortune - wherever *they* got it from." He throws the girls a sneer.

"Tell you what, Walter," he continues. "What do you say? You gamble that key and if you win - well, you get the lot back you've lost, as well as keeping the key. But if you lose - I get the key, but you *still* get

her task, she would never get back to Mum and Josh. The delicious smell of hot chocolate wafted up from downstairs, interrupting her thoughts.

As soon as Tom came into the room, Fran knew that she had made a terrible mistake. The smile was gone. There was nothing in his eyes but contempt - and greed - and it wasn't a cup of chocolate he was holding in

The owl turns his neck
the WHOLE WAY ROUND.

He shouts at Flap, "WATCH WHAT YOU'RE DOING!
Use your bat's sense to see where you're going!"
Flap feels embarrassed.

He's had quite a fright.
He blinks and squeaks in the night.

And when he makes his squeaking sound
Suddenly he knows what's around.
When the noises he makes echo back to him

He knows what's behind and in front of him.

Flap feels braver and more aware
But thinks the owl was a bit unfair!
Flap takes off on wobbly wings
Still thinking of sunlight and daytime things.

bearded man who seemed to chant something, but I couldn't hear anything he said. Then the old man disintegrated and the ashes covered the poor man, who began to shrink. He ended up a few inches high and scurried towards a mouse hole.

"Gunpowder. Treason. And Plot," came the menacing whisper. "GF. Surely you know

everything back that you've lost. Now that's a good deal, isn't it?"

"No, no," cries Molly, holding the key behind her back. "It's ours."

"I think that's a very generous offer of Mr Borwick's," says Merrick. "Sounds fair to me."

The girls stare at him.

They don't understand what is going on and neither do the air fairies chattering outside.

Walter looks tired. "Well, I suppose - I have lost a lot," he says. "And I need to try to win it back. So - you're on, Rufus."

The girls look heartbroken. As the men

start playing 'find the lady', Molly whispers to her sister and the two of them slip outside again, with the key of course.

"Where are we going?" says Griselda.

"I don't know," says Molly. "Maybe we should go and hide in **St Helen's**."

Just then, they hear Merrick.

his hand, but the dagger he had used to poke the fire.

"I'll have the weapon," he said coldly.

"What weapon?"

"The sword you got under your cloak. The sword you jabbed Tom Ingle with when you came in."

"And if I don't give it to you?"

Tom Campion stepped forward. Fran could

Little Flap enters
St Sampson's Square,
The spirit of St Sampson
still lives there.

Not another ghost!
Flap's heart can't take it.
"I hate the dark! I'm not
going to make it!"

the most famous man in York's history? Look at the blackened ceiling. This is one of the many places under York where Guy Fawkes practised with his explosives before going to blow up the Houses of Parliament." Grim came closer.

"The papist plot was just a cover. Blowing up the King was the only way to avenge –

Where are you two off to?"

'Daddy's going to lose everything," says Molly.

'He'll get his pig back," says Merrick. "He'll just lose the treasure. Trust me girls - I know what I'm doing. Come on - let's go back inside and put that key on the table."

He takes them into the tavern.

The children and all of us watch as their father loses yet again. Rufus grabs the key, excitedly, the nasty greed looming in his eyes. "Time to go home," says Walter. "Well, at least I've got everything back. Come on girls."

feel the heat from the dagger blade on her face. "I'll mark you with this."

"Sandy said you were loyal. He said you'd be true to the end!"

"This is the end! I'm just a man with a living to earn. If the King's in, then I'm a King's man, if it's Parliament's turn..."

Fran took a pace back and reached into her cloak.

"Give me the sword, girl. I don't want to hurt you...I swear I'll let you go...on my honour..."

His voice wheedled but Fran could tell that he was lying.

"What will you do with it?"

"Sell..."

Fran threw back her cloak and drew the sword in one movement. She was amazed how light it felt in her hand. Tom lunged forward with the dagger, Fran flicked her wrist and watched with horrified fascination as her sword point slid deep into Tom's dagger arm, just below the shoulder. It took no effort at all.

He bellowed like a bull and rushed on her.

and return to life – Guy Fawkes's great, great, great, great grandfather, Gregor Fawkes, who was a wizard. Many years earlier, James I of Scotland had tricked and trapped Gregor and had him burned to death for the crime of using magic. When Guy found out about the powers his ancestor possessed and realised he could put them to his own use, he decided to take matters into his own hands. He found out he had to kill the King to bring Gregor back, because the King was the living descendant of James I." Grim stopped less than a metre from me.

"I, a poor member of the Minster security force, found out about Guy Fawkes's plans and decided to make a little money from the discovery. But you saw what happened to me and here I am still, 400 years later. And here you are, the prophesied one. Come to put things right."

"But I don't understand...prophesied one? Why me? What does that mean? What am I supposed to do?"

"If you want me to show you," says Merrick to Rufus, "the box can't be far away from where that key was. I can take you there."

"Hold on," says Rufus. "I don't trust you - you might try and rob me, might want the treasure for yourself."

"Well then - why don't we all go together,"

says Merrick. "You trust your friend Walter, don't you? And these two."

Rufus mumbles something, then agrees. They set off in the direction of the forest. The air fairies cannot wait to see if Rufus will find the box and what will be in it when he does.

Fran pulled the sword clear and staggered back. The low sill caught her just behind the knees and she fell backwards out of the window...

Into a snowstorm. She was lying flat on her back, gasping for breath and looking up at a sky filled with snowflakes. It sounded as though a crowd of mad old women were cackling at her and prodding her with bony fingers. Something wriggled underneath

her. The houses marched past on each side in slow procession.

Fran pulled herself upright. Slowly it began to sink in. She was sitting in a cart full of geese, trundling through **St Sampson's Square**. Miraculously, the sword was still in her hand. The driver turned round.

"You all right lass? Had a falling out?" He smiled slightly at his joke. "Strange times,"

he mumbled to himself. "Want dropping somewhere?"

"Back in my own time would be good," Fran thought bitterly.

"Only I'm going back to Fulford. I'm going past St Mary's Castlegate to pick up my boy, if that's any good to you."

"Great," thought Fran, "that's where I was supposed to meet Mum and Josh. I'll only

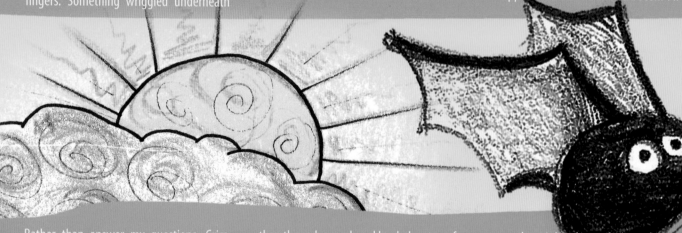

Rather than answer my questions, Grim began to move even closer. I backed away. Then I heard a scraping noise. Suddenly, bricks flew out of the wall next to me, hammering into Grim. Before I knew what was happening, Snickel's paw was around me, throwing me up onto his back. We leaped through the hole he had made and

then through a crack and landed on top of a pipe.

I heard a huge roar of frustration from Grim who was unable to follow us.

My breathing slowly returned to normal as Snickel made his way along the top of the sewer. I felt huge drops of rain on my head. Up through a manhole above me, I could

see the night sky and the tower of **St Helen's Church** that I had looked at from Betty's Tea Room window only a couple of hours before. The storm was still raging, but more than anything I wanted to be up there, on the street, not down here, trapped under the ground. I badly needed to see my dad and my sister again. Even Charlotte

As we reach the forest, it is so dark only a few stars and Merrick's lantern light our way. There, in a clearing ahead, is a wooden basket.

"That wasn't there before," says Molly.

"The treasure is always there if you know where to find it," says Merrick. "All yours,

Borwick. Now it's important that you know what you want to be in the box before you open it."

"I want gold," says Borwick. "Gold that burns brightly and flies out in all directions."

He kneels beside the box and unlocks it, his

hands shaking with eagerness. As he throws back the lid, a huge dragon, bright gold and twice as big as the box, springs out and launches himself in Borwick's direction! Borwick screams and runs out of the forest as fast as he can. The dragon chases after him and breathes hot flames that light up the night sky. Borwick doesn't

be four hundred years early."

"Is that your son?" said Fran, being polite.

"No. Just some lad looking for a job. There'll be plenty of them in York today."

They turned into **Feasegate**, along Spurriergate, then down **Nessgate** to **St Mary's Church**. Fran sat in the cart, clutching the sword to her chest, desperately trying to work out what to do

St Sampson hears,
his laugh makes Flap stop.
"It's not funny! I'm giving all I've got!
It's all right for you ghosts
that walk by night!
I miss the day
and the warm sunlight!"

Sampson stops laughing.
"Brave little one,
My name in Hebrew means *the sun*.
Although at night you
think you can't see,
The sun is there,
you must trust me ."

Flap feels better
and goes on his way.
It's true that the sun rises every day.
And Flap soars up on his little wings
Thinking of daytime
and night-time things.

would do.

I felt so depressed. I was sure I was running out of time. But I had no energy. All I could was to sit, exhausted, on Snickel's back.

At a junction of pipes and cables, Snickel squeezed through a gap in a wall. We stop running until he gets to the **Church of St Mary's**. The dragon flies onto the roof of the church and turns to stone.

Back in the forest, Molly and Griselda are puzzled. Merrick explains, "I knew that Borwick wouldn't find treasure and he'd get a nasty shock when he opened the box, and

I reckon the unicorn knew too - that's why she let you find the key. Borwick's heart was full of greed. Now, if you children had found the box and opened it - it would have been a different story."

As he says this, they look around for the box, but it has vanished.

"Money can't bring you happiness," says Merrick. "I should know - that's why I'm so cheerful, after all - I never have any!"

"I suppose," says Walter, "there are more important things." He looks at his two daughters. "It's time we went home."

Molly and Griselda look at

next. As they approached the church, the geese seemed to get excited. Fran decided she'd had enough of geese for one day.

The new boy was standing just inside the churchyard, leaning over a gravestone - there was something vaguely familiar about him.

As the driver brought the cart to a halt, the boy came running over. He glared at Fran.

Flap knows the hour is very late
As he flaps on to Spurriergate.
The city is strange in the dark.
He has only ever known the park.

Flap sees the traffic lights ahead
Flashing green and amber,
then bright red.

Flap doesn't know what they mean.
When's it safe? On red or green?
Flap's in trouble - he's come so far
But he can't find where
the other bats are.

He flies in circles and
starts to squeak -
Then **St Michael** appears
in the street.

The saint looks up,
holds out his hands,

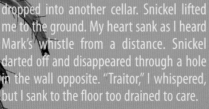

dropped into another cellar. Snickel lifted me to the ground. My heart sank as I heard Mark's whistle from a distance. Snickel darted off and disappeared through a hole in the wall opposite. "Traitor," I whispered, but I sank to the floor too drained to care.

I looked around. There were barrels in this room too, but modern metal ones, with

labels attached to them: "Little John Cellar Bar, **Nessgate**".

After a short while, I thought I heard Snickel returning with Mark and ran, panicking, straight into a sheet of sticky stuff strung between two barrels. Oh no. A web. I was so tangled in it, I could hardly move. I heard a clicking noise above me and froze, my

Merrick. He winks back.

"Thanks Merrick," they say.

"Hey, listen," says Merrick, as they set off. "A word of friendly advice, Walter, don't play cards with Rufus any more. He always cheats."

"What you doing with my father's sword?"

Fran felt as though she had been hit by a bolt of lightning. Scarcely daring to hope, she climbed down from the cart. "What's your name?"

"Jamie Gribham. What's it to you?"

It was suddenly dark in the churchyard, as though the sun had gone behind a cloud.

Fran pulled the sword belt over her head.

"Your brother Sandy asked me to give it to you! He said you'd know what to do. Take it, please!"

Fran suddenly felt faint. She closed her eyes...

"Take it!" Fran pleaded. "Take it, please!"

"Don't be silly, sis!" said Josh. "I've got my own brolly, thanks very much!"

A fat raindrop splattered on the pavement

in front of her, and another. As Fran looked up, the world rearranged itself around her. The big department stores settled into their rightful places, and the jewellers' at the corner, and the tall spire of the church.

"You all right, Fran?" Josh was unusually concerned for his big sister.

"Fine."

They stood, listening to the rain pattering

insides turning hollow with fear. I knew what I was going to see when I looked up.

A giant spider. As I watched, one of its spindly legs reached out and plucked a huge fly from another part of the web. Just below the bulging yellow eyes, an opening that must have been a mouth appeared and sucked the fly in. My stomach turned over.

Then the spider's eyes moved down to settle on me. I was terrified. The more I struggled, the more the web held me. I nearly wet myself when a hairy leg curled itself around me and started pulling me upwards. It was much stronger than I had imagined.

"Quick! Give me your arm." I shuddered and

looked down. Stretching out towards me was Mark. What was worse? I looked up at the slowly opening mouth dripping with saliva. At least with Mark I might have a chance. I just managed to reach his hand. He started to pull. Snickel held on to Mark, adding to his weight. I was being pulled apart! Suddenly there was a snap. The

"I guess I've learned my lesson," says Walter sadly. "Tomorrow I'll look for a proper job."

"Well you could always come and be a street entertainer with me," says Merrick. "It's better than chasing unicorns!"

Well, Walter Turnpike goes home a sadder and wiser man and gets a few cross words from his wife for disappearing, but at least he's learned something.

He'll look for work the next day and he won't trust that Rufus ever again! His two little daughters have helped him win back everything and shown him his family is more important to him than anything in the world. And the kindness of Merrick has shown him the value of real friendship and the need to work hard, but to always believe in the magic in you, around you and beyond you.

As I finish my story, I can see a tear in the corner of Jaconetta's eye.

---

on their umbrellas.

"Sis?"

"What?"

"Has anything...happened?"

Fran thought a long time before answering. "Maybe," she said at last. "I'm not sure..."

She pulled a goose feather from her hair.

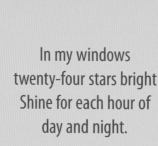

Flap swoons and in his
palms he lands.
"Flap, you made it.
I *knew* you would.
Although you didn't
think you could.

In my windows
twenty-four stars bright
Shine for each hour of
day and night.

If you're scared in the dark,
be brave and say,
'There's always the starlight
to guide my way.'

---

spider's leg broke at mid-point and I went crashing down in front of Mark. I leaped to my feet, pointing the spider's limb at him like a sword.

Mark backed away. "I think you need to hear my side of things, don't you?" he said.

That's a lovely story, Mister Wind," she sniffles.

Then she squeals, "You've done it again! I've lost! I can feel a tantrum coming on!"

The air fairies huddle together, terrified. I don't know why they are - she does this every year. Such a drama queen! And, with that, Jaconetta gathers all her strength and flies away into the distance, wailing.

She'll be back in January!

"Flap, you know now who
and what you are -
A creature who flies by
the light of a star!
In Gaelic, my name means *the Father*
Wherever you are,
you'll be looked after."

Flap smiles as toward
the belfry he flies
Hangs upside down
and shuts his eyes.
Wraps himself up warm in his wings
And dreams of adventures
and happy things.

trail

Now for our final tale, as we continue our air-borne journey with me, the Wind, your all-seeing storyteller. We find ourselves in spring when my breath grows warmer in the returning light of the sun, carrying the scent of new life. The air fairies scatter petals, like messages of joy to the folk of York. At the old castle, **Clifford's Tower**, looking at the distant city, we find Simeon, the 14-year-old baker, whose heart is sad.

"He is in love; he is enchanted," the air fairies tease. I nod and sigh. Simeon dreams of Elise, the Lord Mayor's daughter. They are the same age, knowing each other since childhood. Elise has golden plaited hair, bright smile and often wears fine whit linen. Whenever she walks through Yor she gazes at her reflection in all the sho windows.

Let us enter his dream world with him, an see their story. They meet under the appl

Josh trod on her toe. Hard.

"Josh! Will you just stop it!"

"What? I never did anything!"

They had had a peek at **Clifford's Tower** and were walking past **Fairfax House** on the way down Castlegate to **JORVIK**.

"Mum!" said Fran Marchant. "Can't you do something?"

"Sometimes I wish both of you could just get on, Frances! Is it too much to ask for you to be nice to each other?"

"Both of us? But he was the one who..."

Fran could tell from her mother's expression that it wasn't worth going on. "Frances." Mum only called her Frances when she was in trouble. Mum was always on Josh's side. Just because he was four years younger.

The spider looked ready to leap from its web.

"Come, let's get out of here," said Mark heaving himself up onto Snickel. I hesitated, but I did want to hear his side of things. I kept the spider leg pointed at Mark's back as I pulled myself up after him.

ree in the garden near the Minster. He arries her coat for her, brings her wild lowers from the meadow and reads her adly written poetry. When she is bored, he ells her jokes. He bakes her chocolate cake very birthday. Sometimes she screws up her face and squeals, "Too much cream this year!" but he doesn't care, he loves her so.

Once, she dared him to prove himself by stealing the tallest sunflower from the high walled garden of the house in which lived the oldest woman in York. This old woman had the nastiest temper you can imagine. She guarded her house with a goose that

And a boy. Life was so unfair. Fran tried to work up a decent snivel, but no one was watching so she flicked Josh's ear instead. As he whipped round, she smiled sweetly.

"Horsefly," she said, "Only stings stupid people."

"Gosh!" said Josh, suddenly forgetting his ear. "Look at the crowd!"

The queue stretched round three sides of St Mary's Square - families mainly, with excited children. One little boy was waving a plastic sword; a little girl of about six clung tightly to her mother's hand. Fran felt a twitch of envy. A man dressed like a Viking was working the crowd, swinging his battleaxe around in an alarming way and uttering fierce yells. Josh asked him if it was possible to cut your own leg off, but he

Flash the fox lives in the **graveyard**.

He is called Flash because he can move as fast as lightning.

Flash the fox is always happy. He likes to wag his big orange tail.

He likes to play hide-and-seek in the shadows.

"The other side of this wall," said Mark pointing to a plywood wall in one tunnel, "is **Castlegate House**. 126 years ago it was a Quaker girl's school. Rachel was a pupil there. I was visiting her on our birthday, when a bolt of lightning came through the skylight of the cellar and shrunk us. That's when this never-ending

nightmare began."

In the distance I could see that the tunnel opened into a giant cavern of flickering light. I just knew Grim was ahead of us now, that he was in there somewhere. I had had enough. I might be about to die, but I wasn't going to be pushed around any more. My normal wilfulness was back and it

felt better. Snickel was going quite fast, but it was time to take control. I closed my eyes and jumped.

I hit the ground hard and rolled. For once I didn't mind the spongy surface full of bugs that cushioned my fall. Snickel screeched to a halt a few yards off. Mark slid off and came towards me. Miraculously, I still had

cackled and bit. Simeon was so brave when he risked his life to get that sunflower. When he presented it to Elise the next day, his legs all covered in scratches and goose bites, all she could say was, "Oh, I don't really want it any more. Its petals are falling off."

hurried away without answering. In the corner by Boots, a busker was playing old '70s numbers. Mum began to tap her foot.

Fran was bored.

"How much longer?"

"Be patient," said Dad. "You'll love it when we get in there. There's a Viking sitting on the toilet."

"Can you actually see his bum?" said Josh in a loud voice.

"Why don't you both put on your earphones and listen to some music," said Dad.

"Bugs," said Fran, cringing. "They're called bugs."

"Exactly."

Fran put the bugs of her MP3 player in her ears and pressed the play button. Nothing. That was odd. She pressed it again.

"Good afternoon, Fran," said a voice inside her head, "and Josh. Can you hear me clearly? No need to speak. Just think your answer and I'll hear..."

Fran looked at her brother and mouthed, "Are you hearing this?" Josh nodded. He had one hand pressed to his ear and his eyes were as big as gobstoppers.

"Testing...testing...one...two."

Flash always wins at games
because he has lots of clever ideas.

When he is hungry, he goes into
town to see what he can find.

People think foxes are thieves but
Flash doesn't believe in stealing.

Flash only takes the food that people
have dropped or left behind.

People try to catch him
but Flash is too fast.

the spider's leg and pointed it towards him.

"I'm not going any further unless you tell me WHAT IS GOING ON!"

"Ok. Ok." Mark put his hands up and sat down next to me. "When Rachel and I first came down here, we found Grim hiding in a tunnel. He was quite mad after 300 years in this hell, laughing about how they used to

call him Grim because he was ugly and scarred, but that they should see him now.

"Sometimes he seemed to remember that he used to be a man. I found him weeping once for his lost life. He was occasionally quite helpful, like telling us about a particularly foul white slug that we could eat to slow the decay." Mark paused. "Look,

Sometimes, they talk of their dreams.

"Some day," says Simeon, "I want to see the world. To travel beyond York and see far away places."

Elise smiles. "Will you find treasures and bring back stories to tell me?"

"Perhaps, you will be there too," he says shyly.

"My father probably wouldn't like it," she sighs.

Simeon seems sad at this, so Elise puts her arm round him and reads to him to cheer him up. When she is gone, he pulls at the

petals of daisies, saying, "She loves me, she loves me not."

"This can't go on," says Mirabelle gravely. "So many dead daisies!"

Simeon needs to find a way to win the heart of Elise. His cousin Martha once said that if you wished for something, there were

"Yes," thought Fran hurriedly. "Who are you?"

"Look up at the church. Opposite side of the square. What can you see?"

"Figures...gargoyles...birds..."

"Geese," said the voice. "Greylag geese, actually. Look at the nearest one...that's me..."

Maybe it was a trick of the summer sun but

here's one." He plucked a squirming, greasy white slug from the mud. Grimacing, he sucked it in.

"Ugh." I shuddered.

"Rachel and I didn't know what had happened to us or why we were down here. We had no contact with anyone except Grim. Then one day we turned a corner and

came face to face with a man shrunk like us. I recognised him: Dean Purey Cust from the Minster. He told us that he had found Guy Fawkes's diary hidden in the Minster Library. The diary spoke of wizards, the half-dead and a man, Jim Purecust, known as Grim, doomed to be down here for eternity unless freed by a pure blood

descendant who shared his birth date.

"After much praying, and against his better nature, Dean Purey Cust searched out three sisters, who were said to have, you know, *powers*. The Dean wanted them to help him try and save Grim. Not only because Grim was his ancestor, but also because the diary those in York who could provide a magic cure. He remembers her exact words.

"There is a shop in York - a shop with no name - where the spirit of magic still lives. If you search, you won't find it. Then one day you will stumble on it, like treasure in the dark. The three sisters who run it are dressmakers by the day and witches by night."

Yes indeed - Martha is right. The air fairies nod at me. We know those dressmakers don't we? Their customers are from our world - magicians, elf folk and women of wisdom, seeking cloaks and robes, petticoats and wings to order. A non-magic person might be able to find them - if they required an enchanted spell - but, of course that would be meddling with magic wouldn't it? Is it wise, Simeon, for you to think like this? Simeon feels the chill of my breath.

"Go home, Simeon," I whisper. Evening is

it looked to Fran as though the stone bird turned his head in her direction.

"What do you want with us?"

That was Josh! His lips hadn't moved, but Fran heard his voice clearly in the earphones. This was great...like having a secret telephone.

"We need your help," said the voice simply.

Fran looked at her brother.

"Why us? We're nothing special..."

"Oh, but you are," said the goose. "Close your eyes. Remember."

Fran flinched away. A hand holding a dagger was slashing at her face. Josh was breathless. He could hear running footsteps behind him...getting closer. Both children opened their eyes. They looked at each other with a new understanding.

"Don't be afraid," said the voice. "You have already faced these dangers and overcome them. You have passed our tests. Now, we have another task for you - something so important, you must undertake it *together*."

"Hang on a minute," said Josh. "Who's this 'we'?"

"We are the guardians of the city. We protect it. We guide it through the

recorded the chant of a wizard, Gregor Fawkes..."

"The wizard I saw reflected in the lake earlier," I muttered.

"Yes, him. The wizard's chant suggested that saving Grim would also save all those in the city who had died in troubled ways and were therefore only half-dead, their

ghosts roaming the underground passages of York.

"The sisters gave the Dean a potion that shrunk him for a few hours so that he could find out if it was true about Grim being down here.

"He didn't know who Rachel and I were. Nevertheless, he demanded that we help

drawing in. He is so lost in thought, he has barely noticed the darkness growing. It is not good for him to dwell on this girl. Under my disapproving stare, he shivers and turns up the collar of his coat.

Making his way home, he stops after a few streets at the Church of All Saints, gazing up at the tall **Lantern Tower**. Once it was l... to guide travellers. He imagines it aligh... with a golden and ruby flame. The air fairi... imagine it too. Mirabelle dances wit... delight, so quickly that the sparks fly fro... her red hair. Suddenly a wave of merrimen... from the air fairies sends a ripple of ligh...

centuries. And one of our number is missing."

"Who's that?" - this was Fran.

"Minerva."

"Minerva who?"

Josh broke in, "Goddess of wisdom, dummy. We did Roman Gods at school. There's a statue of her on a wall near the Minster."

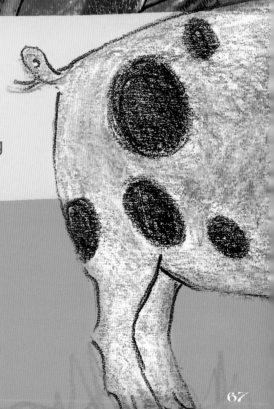

Flash likes to visit his best friend.

His best friend is Petunia the pig.

Petunia is a Princess.

She lives with her father, King Eadwig, in the Kingdom of Swinegate.

Petunia can have just about anything she wants.

him. The Dean seemed a man who was used to being obeyed, so we told him where to find Grim. That's when we started to find out what was going on. Grim was..."

Mark's voice faded as he turned towards the cavern. He stood up. "Come, I think we have to get you in there right now."

"No, not until you tell me what my role in all this is... I won't be used any more!"

"No more time. If you don't follow, you will never know," and he was off faster than he had ever moved before. I caught up with him just as we reached the entrance to the cavern. I looked up. It was amazing. Sort of cool.

The cavern was huge and lit as though by a

like a shooting star, beaming through the dark. Simeon blinks. He is tired - he must be seeing things. Or is it a sign? For today is the day of Valentine, the angel of love. It must be a sign! He hurries on, excited.

"Go home, Simeon," I call to him, but he wants to look for that shop of magic. His absent-minded journey leads him to a stretch of ancient stone wall and a carved wooden door he has never seen before. A strange feeling comes over him - a sense of fear and curiosity all in one. On the door, the words are inscribed, "If your heart be true, ask, knock and find the answer."

Simeon thinks for a moment, then wishes aloud. "I wish for the heart of Elise. She is as beautiful as a shipwrecked mermaid. Her hair is starlight in the day; her voice is like the sound of honey, if honey could have a sound. Will she be mine?"

"For such a poet as you, she can be," says a kindly voice at his side. Simeon jumps as

"If I may continue?" said the goose. "That statue has been the spirit of the city ever since 1801. It has disappeared. Someone has imprisoned Minerva."

"Who?" asked Fran.

"That is not for you to know," said the goose firmly, glancing at the sky.

"Big deal," said Josh. "It's only a statue."

A screech of anguish filled the children's

She can eat hot chocolate pudding all day long.

But Petunia the pig is very unhappy.

"I hate being a pig! I hate mud!

I don't want to be ugly and dirty and sticky.

thousand candles, except there was no sign of the candles, just the candlelight. All around the cavern the ghosts of people dressed throughout the ages stretched up the walls to the distant roof. Here and there were skeletons, but with skulls whose sockets glowed with life.

"Where are we?"

...e sees three women with raven hair, ...herry cheeks and soft blue eyes.

"Welcome, Simeon. I am Laetitia. I spin the ...hread," says the eldest and tallest.

"And I am Clarissa," says the middle sister. "I weave the thread."

"And I am Arabella," says the shortest. "I cut the thread."

Simeon gasps, for he is suddenly upon an empty cobbled street, at the door of a finely painted dressmakers' shop. Its window is filled with rainbow cotton, shiny silk, trims of lace, thimbles, pins and needles. The

...ears. "You are young," said the goose, ...controlling himself with difficulty. "You do ...not understand. Minerva is seated by a pile of books. If she is not released, then the books will die...all of them...every book within the city walls."

Josh sounded doubtful. "How can a book die?"

"Slowly," said the goose. "Letter by letter and word by word...until there is nothing but blank paper, mildew and a memory in the minds of those who have read it. But then the paper crumbles to nothing, and the memory grows weaker...and not just books - every piece of of writing...every newspaper...every advertisement fades away."

"But I like reading," said Fran.

"Then help us. Please."

This was silly. Fran looked at her brother. He was obviously hearing this stuff, so maybe it wasn't so silly after all...but on the other hand...Josh made up Fran's mind for her.

"Where do we start?"

"By the river." The goose coughed self consciously and said,

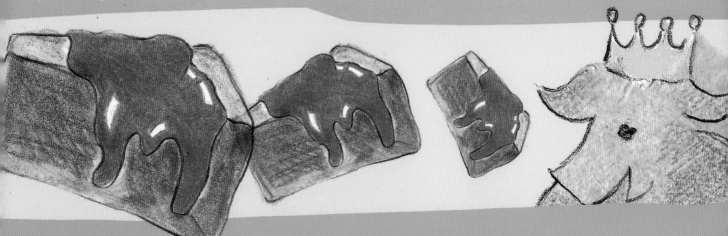

"In the mound under **Clifford's Tower**," Mark said shakily.

In the centre, like a trapped animal, was Grim. His slime dripped noisily onto the stony ground.

"You see those skeletons with the iron helmets hovering over their skulls?" said Mark suddenly. "Vikings murdered in a raid

on their settlement. Look, there are the Roman soldiers we saw earlier. And up there, you see all those white-cloaked people, they're the Jews who killed themselves in Clifford's Tower right above here rather than face an angry mob outside. And you see those grotesque looking..."

Before Mark could continue, there was a

blaze of fire from the floor near Grim that leaped to the roof. The flame slowly transformed into a wizard. It was Gregor, who I'd seen in the lake pictures. His voice thundered out.

"King James I burned me to try and get my powers to use for himself. Then my own flesh and blood, Guy Fawkes, tried to kill

shop with no name.

The sisters beckon and he steps forward nervously, into the shop. I am right behind him, with the air fairies. Of course, the sisters can see the fairies, but not me! I send a breeze to tug at Arabella's hair, just for amusement. Arabella frowns at Mirabelle.

"Listen to those whose voices call,

From the water, land, air and all...

It's a clue to your adventure. A Marchant adventure!"

And then there was a crackling sound, and LifeBoyz, Fran's favourite boyband, blasted in her ears. Fran looked at Josh, but he avoided her gaze.

JORVIK was good, but neither of them could give it their full attention, and they were almost relieved when they came out into the sunshine. It wasn't difficult, getting away from Mum and Dad.

"Just a quick look round the shops, Mum. Just a couple of hours..."

"I want to go to the loo," said Josh.

"Well...all right then. Stick together and we'll see you back at the hotel. Don't be late."

They left Mum and Dad and set off up Coppergate. Neither of the Marchant kids had any idea of where they were going, but they knew that York has hidden pathways of its own, and secret ways of guiding the traveller to the right destination. They just followed their feet. Right at the top of Coppergate, then right again down Piccadilly.

As soon as she saw the sign in Piccadilly,

King James's descendant to reclaim me for his own evil ends. This man," he said pointing at Grim, "became a victim of a fight that wasn't his. Ever since I have waited for the pure Purecust to come and help me complete my task. That time is now! You shall be saved!"

A huge cheer echoed around the cavern. I jumped a foot in the air. I hadn't realised these assorted half-dead could speak. Gregor turned and look straight at me. He smiled and I found myself standing up a little straighter. Suddenly he started to fade, but just before he disappeared I heard him whisper:

Purecust purification begin!

Reverse order to avoid sin.

"Can't stop now, we're closed for stocktaking!" she says to the air fairies and slams the door in their faces.

'Well, how rude!" exclaims Mirabelle, dusting down her wings. We cluster around the keyhole.

Simeon makes his way into a room full of shadows, bright tapestries and flickering candles. Cobwebs hang from the ceiling and brush his coat as he passes, making him squirm.

"Oh, they're not real cobwebs, just cotton wool ones, for effect," says Arabella, laughing.

"Liar," says Mirabelle, "she's just too lazy to do any housework."

"Hush, child," I breathe. "Let's hear what they have to say."

The air fairies know that not all witches are wicked, so are the sisters good or bad witches? We shall see...

"Well, Simeon," says Laetitia. "We know

Fran knew they were heading in the right direction. "A Marchant adventure," the goose had said. She winced at the dreadful pun. They went through the iron gateway and down the steps, the rumbling traffic fading behind them.

Ramshackle. That was the word for the **Merchant Adventurers' Hall**. The pale stone walls were patched with areas of thin

I stink like a skunk.

I want to be like a proper princess.

I want to be clean and pretty and smell like roses.

You are quick and clever and have a bright orange tail.

Gregor had gone, but as he finished his chant a low rumbling began and the ghostly crowd began to advance on Grim. He cried out in terror as they marched, strolled, ran, flew, leaped and floated right into him, each disappearing into his disgusting body with a squelch. Grim's cry of terror increased and he started to grow and grow. Grim's cry became a deafening roar. He thrashed around and the cavern began to collapse, huge rocks falling everywhere.

The whole world was crashing in on me. I was only half aware of Snickel grabbing us from nowhere and stampeding through the dust and rubble into another tunnel. Then

you wish for love with all your heart."

"And we know your heart is true," says Clarissa.

"But we want to hear you ask us nicely," says Arabella.

"I was wondering," he stutters. "Would it be possible that three such lovely ladies as

yourselves could brew a love potion?"

"Well, since you ask..." says Laetita, holding out her hand. A bottle filled with pink potion shimmers into it.

"Know this," says Clarissa. "Your wish is only the beginning - if it comes true, it may turn into a curse. Are you willing to risk that?"

"He must," says Arabella. She conjures a glittering picture of the fair Elise before his eyes.

"She is a proud girl," warns Clarissa. "And her heart may already be full of the love of money."

red brick; Fran could see the ghostly outlines of doors and windows, long since filled in.

There was no one in sight. They were standing on the riverbank, watching the Foss as it rubbed its shoulders against the shingle banks and tree roots and the lost amber beads and the bones of Baltic traders. Half a dozen geese paddled aimlessly underneath the bridge; a

I am stupid and smelly and dirty."

Petunia grunts sadly to herself.

Flash has a plan.
He will make Petunia happy and glad to be a pig princess.

He will use his quickness
and his cleverness.

First of all, Flash gets a big sack
and ties it to his back.

we heard the giant thud of a huge Grim echoing all around us. He was still alive – and moving.

"Mark, you have to finish the story," I pleaded desperately.

Without warning, we emerged through a hole into civilisation. I couldn't believe it. There was a railway of sorts, some houses

that looked as though they were from an ancient village, and people frozen solid in the middle of doing things. Then I remembered coming here earlier with my stepmother. It was the **JORVIK's** underground Viking village. Obviously closed now. Snickel set us down.

Mark frowned and looked back the way

"But there's no harm in trying," says Arabella hastily, "and for all this advice, son, it'll cost you a gold piece."

Simeon is shocked. A whole week's wage!

"Magic is hard work," says Laetitia. "Isn't she worth it?"

His precious Elise. Well, of course she is worth it. The younger air fairies sigh at how much the baker loves her. He hands over a gold coin. Laetitia throws the coin upwards and a giant cash register appears, leaps into the air and snatches the coin into the mouth of its drawer.

---

moorhen nod-nodded its way across to the opposite bank.

"What was that rhyme again?"

"Something about voices calling from water, land and air..."

Fran was worried. She was thinking that maybe they were on the wrong track...maybe this whole thing was a kind of daydream, but then she remembered the

sword... Josh was pointing.

"Look!"

The geese had formed into a line and were swimming purposefully downstream towards them.

Fran had never been too sure about swans and geese. They looked beautiful all right, floating on the water, but someone had

once told her that they could break your arm with one blow of their wings...

The geese were opposite Fran and Josh now, keeping position against the current. Children and geese eyed each other uneasily, and then, as though at an unspoken signal, the six geese turned in towards the bank and began to wade ashore. Then a seventh appeared, high in the air above the bridge, swinging showily

we'd just come. He muttered to himself something about "wrong order..." But then he started to talk again.

"Guy Fawkes's diary apparently indicated that his ancestor, Gregor, was a white wizard. Long ago, a number of these white wizards kept the world in order. Among Gregor's responsibilities was helping those

who died troubled – or unnaturally if you like – to move on from being half-dead to being properly dead.

"Both King James and Guy Fawkes wanted his power. Having control over people's fate in the afterlife would have made them very powerful – and very rich. When Jim Purecust – Grim – found out what Guy

73

Then Clarissa holds the door for him and all three sisters curtsey goodbye.

"What if I need to find you again?" he falters.

"You won't," says Arabella. "*We* will find *you*."

Simeon feels faint all of a sudden, as a blinding flash of light takes hold of him and drives him at lightning speed backwards Then, there he is in front of the **Merchant Adventurers' Hall**. For a second, through the darkness, he thinks the **unicorn on the gate** is prancing and dancing before him.

from wing tip to wing tip, and landing in a flurry of foam.

"Water, land and air," whispered Josh.

The seventh goose shook the water from its feathers, walked up to Fran, and began to talk. It was obvious that whatever he was saying was making perfect sense, but the children could hear nothing but a series of hisses and grunts and squeaks.

"The headphones!" said Josh. "Put them on!"

"...it has already started," the goose was saying. "There are fourteen misprints in today's Evening Press and the sign near **Clifford's Tower** reads C R P RK."

"What do you expect us to do about it?" said Fran crossly. "We were told you would help us."

"The truth is often muddier than a river

after rain," said the goose. "You must puzzle it out for yourselves. There is one who will set you on the right road:

> *"He hunts the rooftops never heard*
> *And ever stalks a little bird."*

"And will he help us?"

The goose made a stifled little noise which Fran interpreted as a laugh.

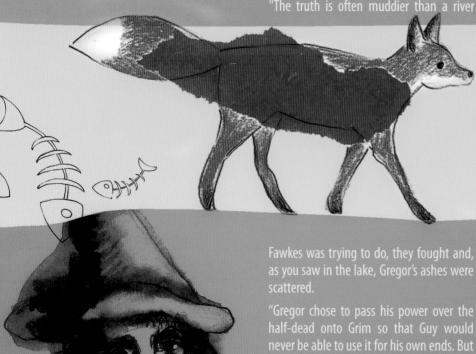

Fawkes was trying to do, they fought and, as you saw in the lake, Gregor's ashes were scattered.

"Gregor chose to pass his power over the half-dead onto Grim so that Guy would never be able to use it for his own ends. But because Grim was a bitter and unkind man – he wasn't pure of heart and spirit –

Gregor's chant to transfer the power to Grim didn't work properly. Ever since, Grim has been trapped down here, kept alive by the magic in him but rotting, going slowly mad and waiting...for you."

"For me?"

"It's like a circle that's been broken in half. Grim and you are two halves of the *same*

The next day, we follow Simeon as he makes his way to his favourite spot in the Minster Gardens. The potion is in his pocket. He has read the instructions. As he walks, the air fairies pull on his coat tails and call to him, "Simeon, be wise, you cannot win the heart of the one you love with magic. Free will must be so!"

Mirabelle sends a shower of glitter onto the little **red devil** on Stonegate, so that he comes alive and whirls round at top speed, joining our procession for part of the way.

"Free will must be so!" giggles the red devil, merrily, spinning all the town signs round in the wrong direction. The air fairies begin to argue with him for trying to lead people astray, and Mirabelle sends him back to his perch with a shake of her head.

"Never trust a devil, no matter how charming," she says.

As Simeon enters the garden, he sees her and they greet each other. When they have

"Maybe. It depends on his mood. Good luck!"

And without another word, the goose turned and flung himself into the air. The others followed, and their wingbeats faded until the children could hear nothing but the chuckling sound of the river and the dull rumble of traffic on Piccadilly.

Fran was getting to know the city by now.

Then Flash goes out to see
what he can find.

Flash goes to the river where the
boats are coming in.

All the people shout,

"Catch that fox!
He wants to steal our fish!"

An angry fisherman with
a bushy black beard throws
a lobster basket.

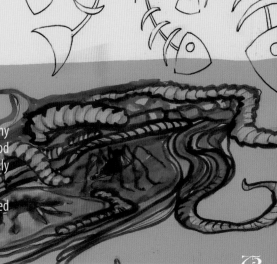

circle. He needs you to complete the circle because you are of the same blood *and* born on the same day. Grim has the magical power to free the half-dead, but he needs to be pure to finish the process. You have, well, you have that purity, because you're a child. So only together can you and Grim help those who are trapped between life and death." Mark paused.

"I'm not sure Grim really understands any more. He just remembers that a true blood descendant must give themselves willingly to him so that he can be free…"

Give myself to Grim. I shuddered. I realised Mark was still talking,

talked for a while, with all of us air spirits watching and wondering, Simeon plucks up the courage to offer her the love potion. How will he get her to drink it? Then he has a bright idea.

"I have a present for you, Elise," he tells her.

"Is it a jewel?"

"No."

"Is it a necklace?"

"No...it's a magic potion...it will bring you whatever you wish for."

The air fairies are whispering among themselves - "What a liar is that boy, he will pay the price for sure."

They turned into Merchantgate and then left again over **Foss Bridge**. Josh looked down at the river, but the geese had gone. Fran was way ahead of him, striding past The Blue Bicycle.

"Hang on!" Josh shouted. "Wait for me!"

"Hurry up then!"

"You know where to go, don't you?"

"I've got a pretty good idea."

Josh wished that Fran would slow down a bit. What about those two houses in the **Shambles**? The ones that leaned out over the road? Josh wondered if you could reach out of an upstairs window and shake hands with your neighbour on the opposite side of the street.

"There!" said Fran triumphantly, as they walked into **King's Square**.

For a moment Josh thought it was a real

Flash only takes what people throw away.

Quick as a flash, the little fox catches the basket and puts it in his sack.

Flash sees a pile of fish bones rotting on the riverbank.

Flash only takes what people leave behind.

Quick as a flash, the little fox puts the fish bones in his sack.

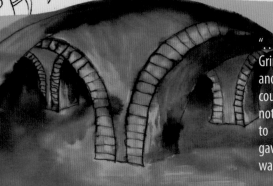

"...when Dean Purey Cust approached Grim nothing happened. He wasn't the one and there didn't seem to be anything he could do. He was a good and kind man, but not the right person to end this. So he had to use the rhyme – or spell – the sisters gave him to return to the surface in case he was unable to help Grim. I don't think he

liked saying he wasn't pure, but the sisters said their spell had to be the opposite of Gregor's chant – bit like an antidote. We never saw him again, but at least he was able to tell us what was happening down here."

The pounding of the giant Grim got closer and then seemed to recede, passing by us in another tunnel.

Elise recovers from her disappointment when she sees the potion. "Oh what a pretty drink," she exclaims, and drinks it, thinking about her wish.

Then she begins to choke. "What is this?!"

"It is a love potion, for you Elise," says Simeon. "And if you will give me your heart,

I will always be true to you."

Elise stares at him and then to his dismay, and to the sorrow of all the air fairies, she throws back her head and laughs loud and long.

"You!" she says. "A common baker's lad! What could you possibly give me, the Lord Mayor's daughter? I am going to marry the

richest man in York one day - my daddy says so - and that isn't you! Why, you still have flour on your hands!"

"Poor Simeon," says Mirabelle and the air fairies try to fan him with comforting feelings. Suddenly, Elise turns blue before his very eyes and then as pale as curdled milk! She chokes and gasps, "Simeon, help

cat on top of the roof. It looked real enough. Its tail was curled in a question mark and the cat was obviously taking an unhealthy interest in the fat pigeon sitting three feet away.

"'He hunts the rooftops never...'"

"Never mind that now!" said the cat grumpily. "Things are going from bad to worse. The labels on the medicine bottles in

Boots are fading away. People are going in there for cough medicine and coming out with syrup of figs."

"Give us the clue, then," said Josh.

"'Ensnared by bricks and magic strong, Minerva's sentence will be long. Let us free her'.

Have you got that?"

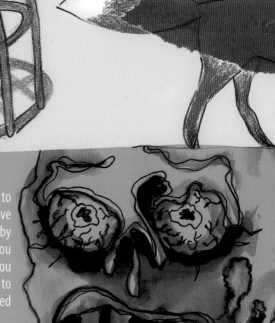

"He's using the big tunnels, built as secret escape routes from the Minster to the river. I guess he can't use the small ones any more," mumbled Mark.

"So, I don't understand. Why have you been trying to get me away from Grim if I can save everyone?"

"When I realised that you were his blood

and born on the same day as Grim, I had to see if you really were the one come to save us. The only way I could test that was by seeing if the rhyme worked. When you couldn't return to the surface I knew you actually were the Pure One. I was about to explain things to you when Grim started chasing us. Then you ran away."

me! Help me - I feel sick!"

Straight away, he picks her up and carries her all the way home, where her anxious parents call for the local quack doctor.

Now news always travels fast in York, almost as fast as me and my messengers, but especially to those sisters who know everything.

"The shame of it!" Arabella is saying to Laetitia, as we gather outside the shop. "Never in all my witching days have we ever made anyone ill!"

"Well it serves us right for interfering with matters of love," says Clarissa. "I did warn you!"

"Oh go boil your head!" retorts Laetitia. "You were as happy as we were to take his money! You know full well how slow trade is these days, with all those wizards making their own clothes."

The air fairies begin drumming against the

The cat said it in such a stern way, like a teacher, that both children repeated it back to him.

"But where do we go now?" said Fran.

"Left down Church Street," said the cat. There was a long silence. "You may go."

Church Street was full of people going somewhere else. Some of them were frowning at their shopping lists, as if confused by something. Others, who looked

Flash is quick and clever.
He races away over the **bridge**.

Flash runs to the market.
All the people shout,

"Catch that fox! He wants to steal our chickens!"

"And it's all gone wrong, hasn't it?" I felt despair again. We were all going to be half-dead for eternity. And in the meantime Grim was now huge. Mark was speaking again, with real sadness in his voice.

"...I know it must have been Gregor who sent Rachel and me down here, that's why I'm still alive after all this time. Like Grim, I'm kept alive by Gregor's magic, but slowly rotting too. He needed us to help him and Grim. When the time came, someone – Rachel – would have to direct Gregor's lightning at a pure Purecust child and someone – me – would have to persuade that child to go willingly to Grim. I had no idea how long we...I...would be waiting

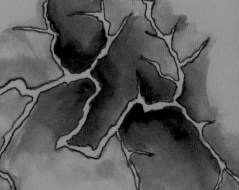

window with their tiny fists. "Witches three, make amends for your meddling!"

Arabella throws open the door. "Stop your chattering you maggoty insects!" she cries. "Your heads are full of sticky toffee nonsense!"

Mirabelle screams at her, "How dare you,

like tourists, were scowling at their guide books, as if they were trying to make sense of them. Fran and Josh looked at each other, eyebrows raised. Only they knew what was happening to the words in the city. And only they could save them.

"We'd better hurry up," said Fran. "Looks like it's getting worse." They stood on the pavement, wondering where to go next.

"Not much of a clue," said Josh in a glum tone of voice. *'Ensnared by bricks'*. The whole city's built of bricks."

"Except the bit that's built of stone," said Fran.

"All right…all right."

"Or concrete…"

"Fran!"

Just then something brushed against Fran's leg. She looked down. It was a cat - a real cat this time - of a soft grey colour, with frosted paws. It looked up at her and gave an urgent little yelp.

"Aren't you beautiful!" said Fran, kneeling down to stroke it.

The cat moved out of reach and then stopped, looking over its shoulder. Fran moved towards it and kneeled again. This

A fat lady screams and throws
a wooden bowl.

Flash only takes what people
throw away.

Quick as a flash, the little fox
catches the bowl and puts
it in his sack.

for that child." Mark closed his eyes for a moment.

"Rachel was only down here for a few days…We were sitting near a grate that we could have got through, but we had discovered we got weak when we tried to go to the surface and would probably die. Suddenly, Rachel got up, turned to me and said simply, "I have to go." Then she walked towards the surface.

"I saw her legs waver as the weakness came on, but she kept going through the grate. She turned with a look of horror. Then I watched the only person I loved begin to disintegrate in front of me, from the legs up to her face. I got to my feet to run after her.

you foolish old thread snapper!"

Arabella looks Mirabelle up and down. "Well better than a badly dressed fairy! Really, Mirabelle, silver satin wings are *so* last century!"

At this, Mirabelle is speechless with horror! But just as she is getting ready to retort, who do we see but an angry Simeon,

standing in front of the shop. Some of the air fairies have led him back...

"Fight, fight, fight!" cry the younger air fairies eagerly.

"Simeon!" cries Arabella, a glint of annoyance in her eyes at the air fairies. "Do come in!" With that she whisks him inside

with a snap of her fingers, the door closing on all of us once more. I scrunch myself up against the window so that I can eavesdrop better.

"What have you three wicked women done?" Simeon asks.

"Well, flattery will get you nowhere,"

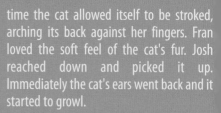

time the cat allowed itself to be stroked, arching its back against her fingers. Fran loved the soft feel of the cat's fur. Josh reached down and picked it up. Immediately the cat's ears went back and it started to growl.

"All right! All right!" said Josh. "Just trying to be friendly!"

He put the cat down and it trotted on again, pausing at the corner. There was something

He sees a heap of chicken feathers sitting in the gutter.

Flash only takes what people leave behind.

Quick as a flash, the little fox puts the feathers in his sack.

But just before her head shattered, she shook it as if to say, 'Don't come,' and then mouthed, 'Later'. The ash that was once her slowly rose in the wind, turning into tiny multicoloured stars as it swept up to form a new statue high on the Minster. It was from there she was able to direct the lightning towards you."

I thought for a moment, then asked, "So, if I'm that child, why did Tom Adams get sent down?"

"It was a mistake. Like the Dean he was a Purecust descendant, but the wrong one. I remembered the chant the Dean had used and helped him to escape."

We sat in silence for a few minutes while I

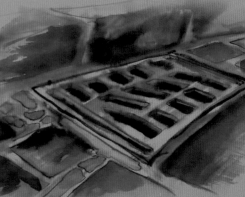

eplies Arabella. "All we have done is what you wanted."

aetita says, "Yes, you wanted to meddle with magic. Of course we didn't think it would make her ill, but you should have read the small print on the instructions."

Clarissa frowns at her two sisters. "What we

about the way it looked at them...like an invitation.

"He wants to take us somewhere," said Fran. "Come on."

The two children followed the small cat down Swinegate. It trotted along confidently, twitching the tip of its tail, which is the sure sign of a cat that knows where it is going.

Then, without warning, it sat down on the

pavement and began to clean its whiskers.

"Is this it?" said Josh, looking along the deserted street.

The cat got to its feet and came to Fran and Josh in turn, receiving a stroke from each of them, and then it simply walked out into the middle of the road and disappeared. Not instantly, like the popping of a balloon, but as though there were an invisible cat

flap there. The head disappeared first, then the front legs, and then the rest of it, leaving only the tip of a grey tail, which twitched for a moment, and was gone.

"I think we're here," said Fran. They were standing outside **an imposing structure built entirely of red brick**.

"Here...Fran!" said Josh. "Look at this!"

Some of the bricks were embossed with

Flash is too quick and too clever.
He jumps over a wall and is gone.

Flash runs through the **church**.

All the people shout,

"Catch that fox! He wants to
steal the holy wine!"

tried to understand everything that Mark was telling me. It was starting to fall into place.

"Mark, supposing what Gregor said about reversing the order means that instead of me having to purify Grim *before* he starts helping the half-dead that I can do it after. That I can still do it."

Mark looked at me. "Would you take the risk?" I thought about the disgusting white slugs I would have to eat for eternity. I took a deep breath.

"What have I got to lose?" I hesitated. "But one question, why did Grim show me his story in the lake?"

"I don't know. Maybe, despite his madness,

did was wrong, Simeon," she says. "We never meant for the potion to make anyone ill. We just thought it would give you the courage to approach the young lady."

"So you knew the potion wouldn't make her love me?" Simeon stares, still angry.

"No one should expect such a thing!"

Letters of the alphabet - not all of them, but a band at about waist height. Most had just two letters, but some had as many as five or six.

"'Ensnared by bricks and magic strong,'" Josh murmured.

"'Minerva's sentence will be long'! Sentence! It's a pun!" Fran shouted.

"It's a code!" said Josh. "Have we got

The priest gasps and throws an empty bottle.

Flash only takes what people throw away.

Quick as a flash, the little fox catches the bottle and puts it in his sack.

Racing outside, Flash sees some flowers lying on the steps.

Flash only takes what people leave behind.

Quick as a flash, the little fox puts them in his sack.

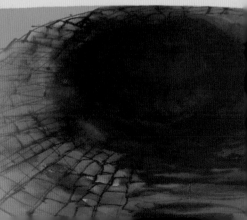

he knew you were the Pure One who could free him. Maybe he thought if you understood his story you would *willingly* help him and the other half-dead become fully dead."

I realised I had to help end all this misery if I could. "Ok. Let's find Grim. Quickly, before I change my mind."

Snickel once more swept us up and raced through tunnels until, just minutes later, we came to a stop. I looked up.

Stretched out in front of me was a huge, long tunnel. Only this time it wasn't lined with bug-infested earthen walls. On either side were raised pavements and occasional shop fronts. Some were decaying and there

Clarissa goes on. "You do not have the right to bewitch someone to love you! For that would not be true love. You have learned a valuable lesson. For all her beauty, Elise is a mean-spirited young lady. In time your heart will heal lad and you will learn that real beauty is inside - not just outside for all

to see and admire. Take this to Elise. It should cure her. And remember what I have said."

She holds a tiny yellow potion in her hand.

"What about my money?" says Simeon, feeling a little foolish now.

"Oh, very well," sighs Laetita and draws a gold coin out of air. "Take this coin. Invest it wisely, baker lad."

"Do indeed invest it wisely," says Arabella. "For I see you have a great future ahead of you, Simeon."

"In a year or less you could be the best baker in Yorkshire," says Clarissa, "and you may

anything to write on?"

"Only that leaflet from JORVIK."

Fran pulled it from her pocket. A shower of tiny fragments, like black confetti, fell from it and melted in the warm air.

"Look!" said Fran, as she unfolded it. "It's happening! The letters are melting!"

"ELC ME TO JO V K," it said on the front.

"Make a copy of the letters on the wall,"

said Josh, fumbling in his pocket for a pencil.

These were the letters he wrote down:

    MN RV N C MRSH LLB FR

    WHNS STR ND BRT HR TGTHR TCH M.

As they looked at the letters, their hearts sank.

"Maybe it's a cipher," said Josh. "Like the

Enigma machines in World War 2."

"If it's that difficult, then we're sunk," said Fran. "Perhaps we're meant to read it from right to left."

Twenty minutes later, the leaflet was covered in arrows and doodles, and they were no further forward.

Thinking about it afterwards, Fran realised that it was like looking at one of those 3D

were gaps. But it was as if we had stepped into a deserted street from history. It was the **Stonegate** of a past century, covered over as the level of the city rose.

The temperature dropped. With a sickening feeling I realised that I would soon have to decide if I could willingly let Grim eat me in order to free him and the others. Did I really

believe in this stuff Mark had told me?

Then Grim was there, at the far end of the street, absolutely huge now having absorbed the half-dead. He was at least 50 times my height, filling the far end of the street with his revolting, quaking mass.

"It's time," came the whisper. It was Gregor's voice.

even find true love, but only if you are as wise as **Minerva**, the goddess of wisdom; look at her statue on **Stonegate** and remember us, Simeon. Fare you well."

He feels himself falling backwards, once more transported, this time to the house of Elise. He wastes no time in taking the cure to her, but once she has drunk it, her angry

father banishes him from ever seeing Elise again, because he made her ill in the first place. Poor, confused Simeon.

A year or two went by. Elise grew in beauty but became even greedier for riches. Meanwhile, Simeon found his heart did heal…

So, as we spy on him now through the window, we can see how very successful he has become. Having followed the witches advice, he has invested the money in his shop. He has learned lots of new recipes - bread, cakes and buns that are baked to perfection. Customers come from far and

pictures - the ones made up of thousands of meaningless squiggles, and then suddenly the picture leaps out at you and you feel stupid for not having seen it earlier. That was what happened to Fran now.

"Josh!" she flung her arms round her brother's neck and rumpled his hair.

"Gerroff!"

"What's missing? What letters are missing?"

Josh looked at the list. Then Fran saw the light dawn in his eyes.

"Vowels!" he yelled. "Not a single AEIO or U!"

"It's a simple substitution!"

It took no more than a couple of minutes to solve the puzzle.

MINERVA ONCE MORE SHALL BE FREE

WHEN SISTER AND BROTHER TOGETHER

TOUCH ME.

"That's it then," said Fran. "Let's do it."

They walked up to the wall and each placed a hand on the warm bricks. Nothing happened.

"It's not working."

"Maybe," said Fran, "if we hold hands...sister and brother...together..."

Flash is much too quick and much too clever.
He leaps over the window sills and over the **cobbles** and runs through the square.

I slid down Snickel's stump, and faced Grim. I was terrified, but I moved slowly forward. Grim advanced towards me. The street was filled with a shimmering white light as I approached Grim in awe as much as fear. Then my chest was against the bottom of his smelly mass of slime.

It gurgled and sucked me in…I couldn't

breathe. A moment's panic. Then suddenly physical feeling didn't matter any more.

I saw swirling bright oranges, reds and yellows forming a tunnel with a white flame at the end. All the people we had seen go into Grim in Clifford's Tower swarmed passed me into the flame smiling as if to thank me. Then the flame slowly

wide as his name spreads through York and beyond!

One day, the Lord Mayor holds a town gala and, now that Simeon is so successful, he is forgiven and invited to attend. It is a bright and summery day. Eagerly, myself and the air fairies, dressed in our warmest finery,

watch as Simeon is presented to Elise by her father, in front of the whole town.

"And this," says the Lord Mayor, "is the richest man in the whole of York. Simeon Lundy. Having become the best baker in the whole of Yorkshire. And you, my daughter, shall have his hand in marriage.

Mirabelle gasps and the air fairies chatter, some with delight, some with dismay. I smooth the curls out of my billowy mane - I saw that one coming and now I can sit back and enjoy the little show...

"I would rather not, your honour, if it's all the same to you," says Simeon.

"Yeah," said Josh. "OK."

So that is what they did, and the letters in the wall seemed to shift and glow with a copper coloured light, and both children felt a cool breeze on their faces, and the figure of a woman passed through their minds. She was tall, wearing a blue robe, and there was a crested helmet on her head, and although she looked rather severe, she smiled at them gently, before fading into the afternoon sunshine.

He runs through the gates of the Kingdom of Swinegate, home to King **Eadwig** and Petunia.

He lays down his sack in front of the sad princess.

transformed into Gregor. He held up his hand.

"It's not your time yet, Sarah. Take some of my powers and go back. There are things for you to do in the world now that the wizards are gone."

Before I could respond, Jim Purecust himself floated past me, looking like he had

in the lake pictures before he was turned into Grim. Gregor dissolved into the white flame again and as Jim passed into it there was a huge bang. Suddenly I was lying on the floor and the final gory remains of what had been Grim were falling around me into the gutters of the old street.

"Sarah?"

"What?!" exclaims the Lord Mayor.

Simeon looks at Elise, her hair elegantly glowing and the smile gone from her lips.

"What do you mean, Simeon?" she says in shock. "Don't you love me anymore?"

"You are too proud," says Simeon, "and you did not love me when I had nothing to offer except myself. So I have given my heart to another - her name is Lucy."

With that, he pulls Lucy out of the surprised crowd. Lucy, the clothes peg seller, who has recently become Simeon's secret sweetheart. Well, the Lord Mayor turns red with rage and Elise stamps her foot and cries, but they cannot bully Simon into changing his mind, however much they try.

So in the end, Elise had to marry the second richest man in York, a merchant, but at least she got her wish to travel round the world with him. In time, her beauty faded and they often quarrelled about the money she spent. Now and again they were content but they would never have the secret of true love and happiness.

Later, when they were walking up **Minster Gates** towards their hotel, Fran stopped at a bookshop.

"What are you going in there for?" said Josh. "I'm hungry. It's nearly teatime."

"Just checking," said Fran. She picked up the first thing that came to hand - a large book bound in red leather - and flicked through the pages. The pages were completely

it all began

and t

history of true

She pulls out the basket and puts it in the mud.

Petunia has a throne.

She pulls out the fish bones and combs her muddy bristles.

Petunia has a fine comb.

She pulls out the wooden bowl and puts it on her head.

Petunia has a crown.

She pulls out the feathers and puts them under her bottom.

Petunia has a royal cushion.

She pulls out the bottle and looks into the glass.

Petunia sees herself in the mirror.

She pulls out the flowers. She puts one behind her ear and ties the other on her curly tail.

I turned. Mark was rooted to the spot. "It's over, Mark. It's time to join Rachel."

Snickel whimpered.

"And it's time for you to go home, Snickel." For the first time since I had known him, he purred. He pressed himself lingeringly against Mark and then shot up a slope between two houses, disappearing through an open grate, back to the alleys he used to roam.

At the end of the underground Stonegate Mark and I walked up a passage to our right that curved up to a grate. Through it we could see **Minster Gates** and the Minster.

"The light-coloured statue on the Minster is Rachel," smiled Mark pointing. "I've done what needed doing, haven't I? It's 'later' now, like Rachel said."

"Yes."

"I'm ready."

He hugged me and boldly walked through the grate. He turned. As he disintegrated like Rachel, he showed no horror like his sister, but kept smiling. The ashes of his

Lucy was not as beautiful as Elise but her spirit was happy and the beauty in her heart made her shine. She loved herself so she knew how to share that with others. We air spirits laughed to see Simeon and Lucy so in love and happy. We know that real beauty comes from within.

As you make your journey around the city of York, remember our tales carried to you with a heart full of wishes and may you be protected always by the good spirits, wherever you are. Fare you well!

blank. Fran turned to the title page. Nothing. She looked at Josh in horror.

"Wait!" he said. "Wait!"

One by one the letters returned, like black flowers pushing up through a snowdrift.

"Eboracum," it said. "A History of the Ancient City of York, by Francis Drake Esq."

"Look there!" whispered Fran.

At the bottom of the page, in tiny letters, it said "preferred for this citty by the corage and clevernesse of F and J Marchant."

"F Marchant," said Josh, "That's you."

"J Marchant," said Fran. "That's you as well."

She leaned over and kissed the top of her brother's head, and he didn't mind at all, as there was no one else in the shop, and Fran wasn't a bad big sister really, as big sisters go.

Petunia smells like roses and she feels just like a proper princess.
"Thank you Flash.
You are not only quick and clever, you are the best friend in the whole wide world."

Flash wags his big orange tail.

body transformed into multicoloured stars and rose to the Minster roof. In front of my eyes a new statue formed next to Rachel.

I took a deep breath. It was time to go back and wait for whatever Gregor had in mind for me. I squeezed through the railings and grew instantly to my proper height. It started to rain again and I wandered back to the Roman column where it all began, humming "happy birthday to me…"

Within moments I heard,

"Where have you been, you *wilful* child."

Gregor's summons could not come too soon.

Breadcrumbs Glossary

1. The Minster

The Minster is the Cathedral Church of St Peter and of the Archbishop of York. Built by thousands of people over 200 years (between 1220 and 1472), it is the fifth or sixth building to stand on this site. The very first Minster is thought to have been a small wooden church, built in AD 627. It is now the largest Gothic cathedral in Northern Europe. This grand and imposing structure was built to glorify God and holds one of the most important collections of stained glass in the world.

2. Statue of Constantine the Great

The Minster stands on the site of an enormous Roman fortress, partially excavated in the 1960s. It is believed that it was in this very fortress that Constantine the Great was proclaimed Emperor of the Western Roman Empire in AD 306 by his troops. Constantine was the first Roman Emperor to convert to Christianity and to allow freedom of religious expression throughout his lands. The statue, made of bronze, was erected in 1998 and stands as a symbol of York's connection with a man who changed the course of European history.

3. Roman column

When excavating the Roman fortress in the 1960s and '70s (see 2), archaeologists uncovered a large pillar beneath the Minster tower. The column was reconstructed and now stands opposite the South door of York Minster. Eight metres high, the column was one of sixteen pillars which supported the roof of the fortress's basilica (main room used as a place of assembly). It is possible to see the base of another column, still in its original location, in the Minster undercroft (crypt used for burials).

4. The Queen's Path

The Queen's Path makes up the middle section of Minster Yard, a street that runs around the Minster. This segment of the path was renamed in 1972 after a visit by Her Majesty Queen Elizabeth II. Her Majesty walked from the West door of the Minster to the Treasurer's House, having distributed the Royal Maundy, a traditional payment of coins to elderly members of the congregation who have given service to the church and their community.

5. St William's College

Built between 1465 and 1467, St William's College is named after St William of York, who was Archbishop of York in 1153. The college was originally home to the Minster's chantry priests who, among other responsibilities, took payment in advance to pray for the souls of benefactors after they had died. During the English Civil War, the college was home to Charles I's printing press. The only surviving building of its kind in the country, St William's College is said to be haunted…

6. Sundial

The origins and erection date of the sundial on College Green are unclear, but it probably dates from the early 20th century. At that time, the houses that used to be where the green is now were knocked down to allow Deangate to run through to the south transept of the Minster. The area where the sundial stands was once a busy shopping area, particularly well-known for a dress shop in the 18th century.

7. Elbow Lane (Monk Bar Court)

The origins of the name "Elbow Lane" are unknown or undocumented. One theory suggests that the name comes simply from the fact that the road bends in the middle. What is known, however, is that this street used to be a carriageway at the back of the Red Lion pub and, in the 19th century, the Albion Iron and Brass Works was located here.

8. Monk Bar

Dating from the early 1300s, Monk Bar is one of York's four main gateways or bars and is the biggest of those that survive. The bar was once a self-contained fortress, a guardhouse during the Middle Ages and a policeman's house until the early 20th century. Monk Bar now houses the Richard III Museum (the top storey is said to have been added by the king in 1484).

9. Wild men of Monk Bar

One of the features of Monk Bar (see 8) are the figures that adorn the battlements at the very top of the bar. Known locally as the wild men of Monk Bar, their origins are a mystery. They may date from as early as the late 17th century (after the English Civil War) or it is possible that they came about as a result of the Romanticism of the 18th century. William Hargrove who wrote the "History of York" (a modernised version of Drake's "Eboracum") described them in 1819 as follows: "on the battlements are small figures in a threatening posture".

10. Groves Lane/Roman Road

Groves Lane stretches along the remains of one of the streets that were used during the time of the Roman fortress (see 2). The *via decumana* was situated at the back of the Roman fortress, and led out of the city. (The gate was later moved to the site of Monk Bar.) Part of the actual Roman street can still be seen today as it forms the floor of a small cellar in the Treasurer's House (near the

Minster). In the 1950s a local man claimed to have seen and heard a group of Roman soldiers march along this part of the road. It is said that the group of men were massacred on their way out of the city, 2000 years ago…

11. Lord Mayor's Walk

Originally called Newbigging Street, Lord Mayor's Walk was renamed in the early 18th century. At this time, York's wealthier inhabitants took to strolling on Lord Mayor's Walk to escape the stench of the city and in 1718 they planted trees along its length. One of the modern features of this stretch of road are the numerous daffodils that line its banks in spring time.

12. Moat

The stretch of grass beneath the city walls and along Lord Mayor's Walk sits on the site of the moat that was once part of the city's defences. Throughout the medieval period, moats were rented as grazing land to the freemen of the city.

13. City walls/Robin Hood's Tower

York's original walls were built by the Romans, and then covered by the Viking defensive mounds and eventually the medieval bar walls, which can be seen and walked on today. This particular stretch of wall (from Monk Bar to Bootham Bar) was restored at the end of the 19th century and stands exactly where the walls of the Roman fortress stood 2000 years ago.

The current Robin Hood's Tower was added in 1888-9 and replaced a much older one. The original tower was called the Bawing Tower until the 1600s when it became known as Robin Hood's Tower. Why it was called this is unknown, however legend has it that two of Robin Hood's associates (including Little John) visited the city in the 14th century and borrowed money from the Abbot of St Mary's!

14. Salvation Army building

Designed by EJ Sherwood in 1882-3, the Salvation Army barracks is home to the York branch of the Salvation Army, and is still used by the organisation today. The motto of the Salvation Army is "Blood and Fire" and it emphasises key points of the group's beliefs: "Blood" for the death of Jesus which saved Christians from sin, and "Fire" for the power of the Holy Spirit which helps Christians to live holy lives.

15. Gillygate and the well

Gillygate (pronounced "jillygate") is an ancient street named after the church of St Giles, which used to stand near the Salvation Army building (see 14). The church was demolished after it was made redundant in 1547, but the road retained its name.

Halfway up Gillygate, opposite no 26 where the white cat sits (see 17), there is the entrance to the Exhibition Hotel. Set back from the road is a covered well. This well was rediscovered in 1982 by the Millett brothers

during construction work on the long low building behind it, thought to have once been the stables of the Exhibition Hotel. (The roof of this building is believed to be the only flagstone roof in York.) The well beneath the covering is typical of Georgian wells which are fairly common across the city. At the time of its rediscovery, it still gave up fresh clean water, and as a result a Victorian pump was fitted to the top. However, the pump feature has recently been removed.

16. Torch snuffer (extinguisher)

The torch snuffer is fixed to a building on Gillygate built in 1769. During the 17th and 18th centuries, young men known as "Side Boys" would guide the footsteps of the well-to-do through York. On reaching their destination, they would snuff their torches in order to preserve fuel. Many buildings would have had a snuffer during this time.

17. White cat

The white stone cat that sits above a shop on Gillygate has been there for as long as people can remember. It probably dates from the early 19th century when stone cats were used to keep rats and mice away. It is not one of the Tom Adams cats that can be seen on walls around the city (see 51).

18. Stone arch, top of Gillygate, by Exhibition Square

The stretch of stone wall that runs alongside the Art Gallery and Exhibition Square was once part of the walls of St Mary's Abbey. In July 1503, the walls were broken through and an arch installed in honour of Princess Margaret, daughter of Henry VII. She was the guest of the Abbot of St Mary's on her journey north to marry James IV of Scotland.

19. William Etty

William Etty (1787-1849) was a York-born painter, best known for painting nudes. He travelled widely throughout his lifetime and in 1828 was elected to the Royal Academy. Two of his paintings can be seen in York's Art Gallery. The statue of William Etty, by George Walker Milburn, was erected in 1910.

20. King's Manor

Originally part of St Mary's Abbey (see 25), King's Manor was the Abbot's House and its earliest remains date from the 13th century. During its history, it has been home to the Council of the North; the residence of the military governors of York; a private girls' boarding school; and a school for the blind. It is currently leased by the University of York from the city council and houses the departments of Archaeology, Eighteenth-Century Studies and Medieval Studies.

21. Roman wall

The piece of wall in the car park next to the council offices on St Leonard's Place is the remains of the Roman fortress wall (see 2) which was broken through to make way for the street and its buildings between 1833 and 1834. Over 100 feet of the wall was demolished at that time; more remains can be seen next to the King's Manor.

22. Theatre Royal

In 1744 the New Theatre opened on this site and, under the management of Tate Wilkinson, became the Theatre Royal in 1769. Wilkinson raised the standard of the theatre during his leasehold, however the 19th century saw a steady decline in its fortunes, due to competition from the music halls and, later, the cinemas. The theatre is currently owned by the York Citizens' Theatre Trust. The Gothic frontage was added at the end of the 19th century. Designed by the city engineer George Styan, the roundels are of Shakespeare and some of his characters.

23. Crypt under Theatre Royal

The Theatre Royal is built on the remains of St Leonard's Hospital. Part of the hospital walls are still visible today from the foyer and beneath the theatre are the vaulted undercrofts (lowest storey) of the original building. St Leonard's was once the largest hospital in England – it covered the area between the theatre and the Museum Gardens. Founded in the 10th century by King Athelstan, it lasted for over 500 years, until it was closed in the 16th century during the dissolution of the monasteries.

24. Water fountain outside Museum Gardens

Very little is known about this water fountain, other than that it dates from the Victorian period and was installed in 1880.

25. St Mary's Abbey/Museum Gardens

St Mary's Abbey dates from the late 11th century and was, in its day, a Benedictine priory. The abbey was destroyed in 1539 when Henry VIII dissolved the monasteries to fund his war with France. The ruins of the abbey stand in the Museum Gardens (so-called because the park is home to the Yorkshire Museum). Originally intended for use by members of the Yorkshire Philosophical Society, the gardens became open to paying members of the public after a visit from Queen (then Princess) Victoria in 1835. Both the park and the abbey are open to visitors until dusk.

26. Lendal Tower (Water Tower)

Built in the 13th century, Lendal Tower was originally part of the city's defences. During the medieval period, a chain was strung across the river from Lendal Tower to Barker Tower (see 28). The chain was believed to have been used to stop boats from leaving the city in times of trouble or for not paying their taxes. In 1682, the tower became part of York's first ever waterworks. Water was pumped from the Ouse to the city via pipes made from tree trunks. In its original form, Lendal Tower would have looked more like Barker Tower, but additions to the building were necessary to house the devices used for pumping the water. (It was made taller in the 17th century using stone from St Mary's Abbey (see 25).)

27. Lendal Bridge

In 1860 the foundation stones for a bridge designed by William Dredge were laid, but the incomplete structure fell down the following year. The present bridge was completed in 1863 and designed by Thomas Page, who also designed Westminster Bridge in London. Until 1894, Lendal Bridge was a toll bridge, and the toll houses can still be seen – they now house a café and shop.

28. Barker Tower

A "barker" stripped oak bark for use in tanning, which is the preparation of animal skins. Tanner's Row and Tanner's Moat are nearby and the area near Barker Tower was the centre of York's leather industry. This tower is believed to have been built in the 14th century and, like Lendal Tower (see 26), was also originally part of the city's walled defences. The tower now houses an artist's studio.

29. Lendal

St Leonard's Hospital (see 23) once had a landing area on the River Ouse, called St Leonard's Lendinge. The name "Lendal" originates from this period when the street was known as "Ould Connystrete alias Lendinge Street". It was first referred to as Lendill Street in 1639. Lendal has been home to York's main post office since 1703. It was also once the site of an Augustinian priory where King Richard III stayed in the 15th century.

30. St Helen's Square

During Roman times, St Helen's Square was the site of the main south-west entrance to the Roman fortress (see 2). The double gates would have been flanked by towers and heavily guarded. The square takes its name from St Helen's Church (see 31), which was first mentioned in 1235. However, the square itself didn't come into existence until 1745, when the graveyard of the church was moved to make room for it. Originally a narrow junction, it has been widened twice, lastly in 1929 when the York Tavern (later Harker's Hotel) was demolished.

31. St Helen's Church

St Helen's Church is dedicated to Helena, mother of Constantine the Great (see 2). She converted to

Christianity after her son become emperor of the entire Roman Empire in 312 AD, at the age of 63. She devoted the remainder of her life to the faith by serving the poor and building churches.

The church of St Helen's was built in Norman times but was closed in the early part of the 16th century. It was due to be demolished in the 1550s, but was restored some years later and again in the 1800s. There is medieval stained glass in some of the windows, one of which shows the badge of the "Worshipful Company of Glaziers". During the medieval period, Stonegate housed York's glass painting industry and St Helen's was the glaziers' church.

32. Davygate

The Forest of Galtres lay to the north of York until the mid 18th century, although by then little of it remained. During medieval times, Davygate was the site of the forest courthouse and prison, used to imprison poachers. It is either named after Davy Hall, home to the Larderers who were the gamekeepers of the Forest of Galtres; or it was named after David Le Lardiner, whose father was the Royal Lardiner for the Forest of Galtres in the 12th century. (Lardiner means clerk of the kitchen.) In 1745 Davygate became the new home of the graveyard of St Helen's Church (see 31), which can still be seen today.

33. Coat of arms on no.1 New Street

The buildings on New Street (off Davygate) were built in the 18th century, however no. 1, currently a café, was rebuilt in 1959. The origins of the coat of arms are unknown, although it is possible it was the coat of arms of a bank.

34. Owl mosaic on Davygate

Up on the wall by the recessed graveyard of St Helen's Church on Davygate (see 31 and 32) is an owl mosaic. Its origins and artist are unknown, but it probably dates from the 20th century.

35. St Sampson's Square

St Sampson's Square takes its name from St Sampson's Church (on Church Street). Very few churches in the world are dedicated to the Welsh St Sampson (6th century AD) and his connection to York is unclear. The current building dates from 1848.

The square was home to the Thursday market in medieval times and the last market hall wasn't demolished until 1815.

The Roman Bath Inn, on St Sampson's Square, houses the bathhouse of the Roman fortress (see 2). The sewers which served the baths still survive today and are located under Church Street.

36. Feasegate

Feasegate comes from "Fe-hus gate" which is Old Scandinavian for cow house lane, suggesting it was where cattle were bought and sold. The remains of a second Roman multangular tower were discovered under Feasegate; the first can still be seen in the Museum Gardens (see 25).

37. St Michael's Church

The date the church was built is unknown; however it is believed that a church has stood on this site since Anglo-Saxon times. (The first reference to it was in 1089.) St Michael's was once owned by St Mary's Abbey (see 25), but after the dissolution of the monasteries in the 16th century, it reverted to the crown. In 1821, seven feet were cut off the church to make room for road widening. Between 1872 and 1931, a curfew bell was rung from the tower of the church – no curfew was imposed in the city, but it was customary to ring the bell. The bell tower was pulled down in the 1960s. The church is now home to a café and called the Spurriergate Centre.

38. Nessgate

Part of what remains of York Castle is Clifford's Tower (see 42), which was once the castle keep, or safe retreat and lookout tower. The castle was built by William the Conqueror in 1068. The castle stood on a "ness", which is the Viking word for "triangular headland" – in this case it refers to the triangular shaped land between the River Foss and the River Ouse. Nessgate literally means "ness road" or "road to the ness".

39. St Mary's Church, Castlegate

It is believed that St Mary's was, at one time, one of the largest and most important churches in York. A dedication stone was discovered that dates from 1020, although most of the church is believed to be 12-13th century. The tower and spire were added later, in the 14th century, and the spire can be seen from all over the city. It became redundant as a church in 1958, and is currently used as a contemporary art venue, run by York Museums Trust.

40. Castlegate House

Castlegate House dates from the mid-1800s and was built for the City Recorder, Peter Johnson. It was the site of the Mount Friends' Girls' School between 1831 and 1857.

41. Clifford's Tower

Clifford's Tower is part of what remains of York Castle (see 38). The origin of the name is unconfirmed. Some believe the tower to be named after one of the most influential northern families during medieval times, the Cliffords; others believe the tower is named after Sir Roger Clifford, who was hanged there in 1322. The original tower was made of wood but burned down during the massacre of the Jews in 1190. It was replaced with two more

wooden structures and finally a stone structure in 1246. The tower had two floors and a wooden roof until 1684 when it was damaged by a St George's Day salute that went badly wrong.

Clifford's Tower has been a castle keep, a fort, a prison and a mint. During the 17th century it was a garrison and hence a symbol of authority, and was known to the locals as the "minced pie". One of the most popular toasts of the period was "To the demolition of the minced pie!" The tower is currently owned and run by English Heritage and is open to the public.

42. Fairfax House

Fairfax House was designed by the same architect as Castlegate House (see 40), John Carr, and built in 1762 for the ninth Viscount Fairfax. Part of the building was used as a cinema between 1921 and 1965, and the house is currently home to a collection of Georgian furniture. The house and the collection are open to the public.

43. JORVIK

Between 1976 and 1984, the ruins of a 10th century Viking village were discovered on and around the site of JORVIK. The excavation uncovered the timbers used to build houses, thousands of artefacts, and animal and vegetable remains, all of which had been preserved in the waterlogged ground near the River Foss. JORVIK used the discoveries to accurately recreate a Viking village in incredible detail.

44. Lantern Tower (All Saints, Pavement)

Until the mid-18th century, the Forest of Galtres lay to the north of York (see 32). The forest covered a vast area and extended as far as the city walls. The Lantern Tower of All Saints Church was once used to guide travellers through the forest, which at night was said to be full of wolves and thieves.

The forest probably became the property of the crown during the reign of Henry II and for hundreds of years was the main source of the city's oak (the Merchant Adventurers' Hall (see 46) is framed in Galtres oak). The forest is mentioned by Shakespeare in Henry IV part II and echoes of it remain today in the names of some of York's surrounding villages, such as Sutton-on-the-Forest.

45. Merchant Adventurers' Hall – unicorn on top of gate

The gate to the hall on Piccadilly shows the coat of arms and emblem of the Guild of the Merchant Adventurers (see 46), which includes a prancing unicorn.

46. Merchant Adventurers' Hall

Built between 1357 and 1368, the Merchant Adventurers' Hall was originally a hospital dedicated to the Blessed Virgin. But in 1430 it became the meeting hall of the Fellowship of Mercers (dealers in textiles) and the Guild of the Merchant Adventurers who controlled trade in the city for over 600 years.

47. Foss Bridge

It is thought that a bridge has stood on this site since the time of the Vikings. Nevertheless, little is known about earlier incarnations of the present structure, built in 1811. However, this area around the River Foss was the location of one of the city's fish markets during the 15th century. It was also the site of a quay used by the Merchant Adventurers' Guild (see 46) for loading goods onto ships travelling to the Low Countries.

48. St Crux Parish Hall

The building by Whip-ma-whop-ma-gate was built on the site of St Crux Church and incorporates part of the wall of the original structure. It is a parish room or church hall, which is currently used as a café. Before it was demolished in 1887, the church was considered one of the finest and largest medieval churches in York, first mentioned in the Domesday Book. It is called St Crux due to the fact that the church was dedicated to the Holy Cross, not a saint (crux is Latin for cross).

49. Shambles

York's most famous medieval street is the only existing street to have been named in the Domesday Book. Although much of the narrow road was restored during the 20th century, most of the buildings there today date from the 15th-17th centuries. The name derives from the word "shammels" which were benches on which a butcher's meat was displayed – the Shambles was once a medieval street of butchers. (The benches and meat hooks can still be seen.)

50. King's Square

King's Square is the site of the south-east gatehouse of the Roman fortress (see 2) which was also the palace of the first Viking kings of York in the 9th and 10th centuries. The gatehouse was demolished by William the Conqueror in 1068.

Until 1937, the church of Holy Trinity stood here and the outlines of that structure can still be seen, as can the gravestones.

51. Tom Adams's cat

A black stone cat stalking a pigeon can be seen up on one of the rooftops in King's Square. The cat is the emblem of one of York's architects, Tom Adams, who, as a student, used to add a silhouette of a cat to his architectural drawings

to make them stand out. The cat was created by York sculptor Jonathan Newdick (see 53). Other examples of Adams's cats can be seen around the city.

52. Eadwig Pig

The statue of a pig's head, situated by a restaurant off Swinegate, is called Eadwig Pig after King Eadwig who ruled England during the 10th century AD. The statue is by York sculptor Jonathan Newdick and was named, following a competition, by Rachel Beevers in 1992.

53. Letters on York Central Mission Hall

This meeting hall was built in 1910. At that time, locals paid seven shillings to have either a dedication carved into a stone, or their initials or an acronym of their favourite hymn carved into bricks which were then laid as part of the structure.

54. Stonegate

Stonegate sits on the site of one of the most important roads during Roman times – the *via praetoria*. Its name (first recorded in the 12th century) quite literally means "stone road". For hundreds of years, Stonegate was associated with the book trade and contained many bookshops. Printing presses were also situated there and some newspapers were printed in Coffee Yard.

There are reports of a "hidden street" under Stonegate. Reached from the basements of a number of shops, it is described as being just like a real street with shop fronts and even windows. It is possible that this is the remains of the original Roman road which is known to have been several feet lower than the roads in York today. The "hidden" street is not accessible to the public.

55. Red devil

Stonegate was famous for being the site of York's book trade (see 54) and the red devil is the traditional sign for a printer's shop. Exactly why a red devil should be associated with printing is unknown, although theories abound. Among them is the fact that apprentice printers were (and still are) referred to as "printers' devils". Printing was also once associated with the devil's work and known as a "black art" because unless you were a priest you had no business being able to look into the church's texts.

56. Minerva

As with the red devil (see 55), the statue of Minerva is also associated with the book trade. Minerva is the goddess of wisdom and drama and the sign indicates that the shop was once home to a bookshop. (The bookshop was owned by John Foster between 1580 and 1607 and he was believed to have had a stock of over 3000 books – remarkable for the time.)

57. Minster Gates

Minster Gates was originally known as Bookbinders Alley, and is still home to a respected second-hand bookshop. It derives its current name from its proximity to the Minster Close, where gates once stood.

Snickelway

The word "snickelway" was coined by Mark Jones who wrote a book, "Walk around the Snickelways of York", in 1989, and it has since become part of the city's vernacular. Snickelway means narrow passage and refers to the numerous alleyways in York, such as Coffee Yard off Stonegate.

Although the characters in these stories are fictional, some of the names used are those of real people...

Tom Adams (1937-): York architect well known in the city for decorating his buildings with stone cats.

Dean Arthur Percival Purey Cust (1828-1916): Long-serving Dean of the Minster, after whom the Purey Cust hospital was named.

Thomas Fairfax (1612-1672): Army leader and famed Parliamentarian (Roundhead) who played a crucial role during the English Civil War.

Guy Fawkes (1570-1606): Born in York, infamous religious extremist and architect of the failed attempt to blow up parliament, the Gundpowder Plot, which is still marked today by Bonfire Night.

Chasing the Unicorn

"Chasing the Unicorn" is an actual phrase which means chasing impossible dreams. It is most famously used by Jules Vernes in "Twenty Thousand Leagues Under the Sea" (1870).

Acknowledgements and Further Reading

The York Book, Edited by Antonia Evans, Blue Bridge, 2002

Bartholomew City Guides: York, J Hutchinson and DM Pallister, John Bartholomew & Son Ltd, 1980

City of York Council trail guides (Roman York; The Story of York's Medieval Churches; The City within a City; A Walk through 1900 Years of History)

www.thenortheast.fsnet.co.uk
www.yorkstories.co.uk

In August 2004 City of York council launched The Renaissance Project with funding from Yorkshire Forward. The Renaissance Project goals were to generate external artistic installations of a temporary or permanent nature that would enhance the experience of being in York for both residents and visitors. It was hoped that the project would provide a platform to celebrate the heritage of this ancient city whilst also contributing to community safety and supporting the evening economy.

In September 2004 ENDpapers Ltd responded to the Renaissance Project's call for proposals to York's creative industries and put forward the BREADCRUMBS concept to deliver three things. The first was this book written and illustrated by local people. The second was a series of trails through the city with the start points marked by the work of local artists and connected by reflectors set into the pavements. The third was a transferable model, not only for developing more trails within York itself, but also for providing a methodology to other cities wishing to do the same.

In October 2004 ENDpapers was awarded funding for the project and work began with a delivery date of the end of March and the launch of York BREADCRUMBS in April 2005.

The book involved fifteen people on the creative team alone. The entire project has involved more than fifty people including stonemasons, writers, bureaucrats, engineers, artists, printers, glass manufacturers, potters, typesetters and proofreaders.

The process has not been without its difficulties. But it is testament to the tenacity of many players that York BREADCRUMBS has delivered a book, trails and complete record of progress, within six months. It just goes to show, things can be done quickly, well, and with public and private sector co-operation, once people decide they want them to happen.

We hope you enjoy the York BREADCRUMBS experience whether following the trails in the city or simply reading the book.

Rory McCarthy – **The Renaissance Project**
Magdalena Chávez – **END**papers Ltd
April 2005

Walking through York on the "York BREADCRUMBS" trails

Disclaimer:

York BREADCRUMBS project cannot be held responsible for any personal injury or damage to or loss of possessions that may occur in your choice to take up the challenge of any one of the published walks.

If you have a heart condition or any other medical condition that could have an impact on your walking ability, please consult your doctor beforehand.

Advice:

The York BREADCRUMBS trails direct people by foot through the city centre. They have been chosen with families and safety in mind. York is generally an extremely safe city that is frequented by many pedestrians day and evening and provides a pleasant environment for discovering the city on foot. None of the trails should pose any onerous challenge. Follow simple personal safety advice such as:

- Keep to the prescribed routes.

- Cover up expensive items such as jewellery, personal music players, mobile phones, etc.

- Don't carry valuables unless absolutely necessary.

- Be aware of your environment and those around you.

- A torch, mobile phone and personal attack alarm are useful.

- Avoid dark alleys and ill-lit pathways if you are unfamiliar with them.

Local numbers to phone if you have concerns are:

York Police: 0845 6060247
or **999** (in emergency only)

If you have enjoyed this book, check out our other books that either have a York theme or are for children.

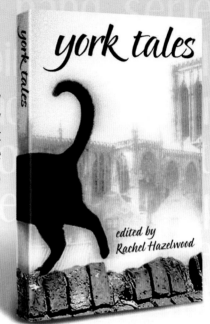

YORK TALES - an exciting new anthology of comtemporary writing presents twenty short stories about everyday life
ISBN 0954324773

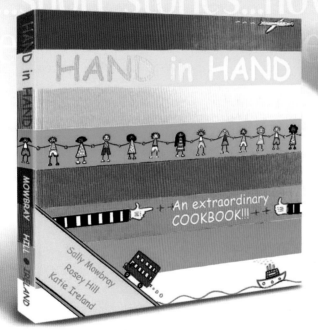

HAND in HAND - a world of a book for both children and adults. With recipes and stories for people of all ages
ISBN 0954324722

And don't miss the *novels of the spirit* in the action packed York Trilogy.

Festival of Angels ISBN 0954324714
Fiesta Latina ISBN 0954324757
and **The Last Supper** ISBN 0954324765

all available from good booksellers and on line at www.**endpapers**.co.uk